This book belongs to:

Shcool 'olidays

CONTENTS

STORIES BY JAMES HENDERSON AND IAN ROBINSON
ILLUSTRATED BY JOHN HARROLD
STORY COLOURING BY DORIS CAMPBELL

John Harrold.

ISBN 0-85079-242-8

RUPERT

THE DAILY EXPRESS ANNUAL

John Harrold.

No 56

Published by Express Newspapers p.l.c., 245 Blackfriars Road, London SE1 9UX

£4·25

RUPERT

One morning Rupert starts to say
He can't think what to do today . . .

Rupert is at a loose end. It is the middle of the school spring holiday and all his pals have gone away with their families. "It's no use," he sighs, as his mother clears away the breakfast things. "I just can't think what to do today!" At that moment there is a knock at the door and Rupert hurries to open it. "What a nice surprise!" he cries. For there on the doorstep stands his old friend, Sailor Sam . . .

and the Angry Sea

But just then Sam, his sailor friend,
Appears and all his troubles end.

"I'm driving down to see the sea,
Perhaps you'd like to come with me?"

"How'd you like to spend a couple of days by the sea?" asks Sam. "I'm off to Cocklesands to visit an old shipmate of mine, called Jem. I've borrowed a car for the journey. Come and see." "What fun!" laughs Rupert. "I'd love to come. Let's go and ask Mummy." Mrs. Bear likes Sam and knows he can be relied upon to take good care of Rupert. "Of course you may go," she says. "A trip to the seaside will make a pleasant change."

He asks his mum, then cries "Hooray!"
As Mrs. Bear says that he may.

RUPERT SEES SOMETHING ODD

Sam starts the car, the trip's begun.
"Goodbye!" calls Mrs. Bear. "Have fun!"

Near Cocklesands they glimpse the sea.
It's rough – although the day's wind-free.

"That's odd!" says Sam. "A false alarm!"
For now the sea has grown quite calm.

"But why are those two fishermen
Still hauling their boat back again?"

In no time at all Mrs. Bear has packed a case for Rupert, and he is on his way to Cocklesands with Sam. Sam explains that his friend Jem is a fisherman who has a little boat of his own. Rupert can hardly wait for the sea to come in sight, but when it does, just outside Cocklesands, the two friends can hardly believe their eyes. Although it is a fine calm day the water looks windswept and rough. Then the road turns inland and they lose sight of the sea for a while.

When they see it again, from a hill above Cocklesands, they are even more surprised, for now it is still and calm! "This is mighty odd," says Sam. "All the boats should be out fishing by now. Yet there's only one in the water and even that's being beached." When they get closer Rupert and Sam can see that the two men who are dragging the boat ashore are soaked to the skin. "Let's find Jem and ask him what's going on," says Sam.

RUPERT HEARS A STRANGE TALE

They go to visit Sam's friend, Jem,
Who hurries out to welcome them.

"How's fishing?" asks Sam. "Stormy seas?"
"Yes," Jem replies. "Though not a breeze!"

"The moment boats put out to sea
It storms and rages fearfully!"

"One tried today, but, as you saw,
We had to winch it back ashore . . ."

Jem is standing at his cottage door when the two chums arrive. He shakes hands and admires Sam's car, but his eyes keep straying to the boat that's just been beached. Inside the cottage Sam asks him what's wrong. "It's plain you're worried about something," he says. "Ay, like all of us here," says Jem, adding, as if to himself, "'cept for one!" "Does it have to do with the sea?" asks Sam, remembering what he and Rupert have just seen. "That it has," sighs Jem.

He sits down at the table and begins to tell them what's been happening . . . "One fine day, the local fishing boats set out to sea as usual, but as they reached the entrance to the bay a great wind sprang up and drove them back towards the shore. Ever since then, no matter how calm it seems, the moment the boats reach the open sea a sudden squall forces them back again. We send a boat out early each day to see if things have changed but it was just the same this morning."

7

RUPERT IS SHOWN JONTY JINKS

"There's something very wrong, I fear,
That threatens everybody here."

" 'Cept Jonty Jinks, who says that he
No longer needs to fish the sea."

"Wake up," says Sam. "It's fine today.
Let's watch the boats down by the bay."

"Hello!" says Jonty Jinks. "Nice day –
At least, for now it looks that way!"

"It's as if the sea was angry with people here," Rupert suggests. "Ay, just so," agrees Jem. "And that's why everyone in Cocklesands is so worried." "All except one, you said," Rupert reminds him. "And there's the very one!" cries Jem, who has been looking out of the window. "Jonty Jinks himself!" The others follow his gaze to see a man who looks as if he's gloating over the idle boats. "Fisherman till lately," Jem adds. "But now he says he's giving it all up."

Next morning Rupert is woken early by Sam. It is a fine day. "They're taking a boat out to test the sea right after breakfast," Sam says. "Let's go and watch." And so a little later the two friends march down to the shore, together with Jem. When they get there two fishermen are pushing a boat into the water, watched by a small crowd. Jonty Jinks is there too, but stands apart from the others. "Nice day," he says, then adds with a smirk, "For the moment, anyway."

RUPERT SEES A SUDDEN SQUALL

The fishermen watch anxiously
As the first boat puts out to sea . . .

At first all's well, but then, oh no!
A sudden storm begins to blow . . .

"Stay there!" calls Sam and hurries to
Do what he can to help the crew.

"No more of that for me!" says Jinks.
"I'll soon be rich!" he laughs, then winks.

The friends ignore Jinks, for everyone's attention is on the boat being launched into the calm sea. As the boat turns towards the entrance to the bay it starts to get rougher, not much, but more than you'd expect on such a fine day. Everyone – except Jinks – watches anxiously. The boat has almost reached the open sea when a groan goes up from the onlookers. In an instant the sea is whipped into a fury and the boat hurled back towards the shore.

"Stay there!" Sam shouts to Rupert, as he and Jem race to where the boat is about to be washed ashore with its crew drenched and gasping. Almost as if it's satisfied with having hurled back the boat, the sea grows calm once more. A voice behind Rupert says, "Makes me glad I can give up fishin'." It's Jonty Jinks. "How can you do that?" asks Rupert. "Surely it's your living?" Tapping his nose mysteriously, Jinks winks at him and says, "Comin' into money, I am. Lots of money!"

RUPERT EXPLORES THE SHORE

As Sam returns Jinks walks away
And Jem asks what he had to say.

Jem seems surprised by Jinks's news.
"What's made him rich?" he starts to muse.

Now that the sea is calm once more,
Rupert decides to search the shore.

Although the tide's a long way out
He sees something splashing about . . .

Jinks stalks away as Sam and Jem return from helping to pull the boat ashore. "Did I see that Jonty Jinks talking to you, Rupert?" asks Jem. "You know, he's none too well liked round here. What did he have to say?" "He was telling me he's coming into money," replies Rupert. "Is he now?" breathes Jem. "I wonder where that's coming from. No wonder he's been going about looking as if he hadn't a care and saying he's giving up the fishing!"

Sam and Jem look thoughtful. Seeing that they have lots of things to talk about, Rupert asks if he may go and explore the shore. Of course he can, he's told. But at the first sign of a squall he must be sure to take shelter. So off he goes, heading for the rocks, where he hopes to find some interesting pools below the high tide-mark. He is almost at the end of the bay when his eye is caught by a wild thrashing and splashing coming from a pool that's hidden by a cluster of rocks.

10

RUPERT FINDS A STRANDED FISH

"A fish!" gasps Rupert. "Goodness me!"
It's been left stranded by the sea!"

"There must be something I can do.
Yes! This pool's big enough for you."

The fish looks pleased and starts to swim
Around as Rupert watches him.

Then Rupert's shocked to hear it say,
"I should have known to stay away!"

Rupert steals up to the pool and peers in. To his surprise, he sees a big fish thrashing about in the shallow water. "Poor thing!" he cries. "It must have been stranded here by the sudden squall." Rupert decides to help the fish. The sea is too far out to risk carrying it to the water's edge, so he starts to look around for a bigger pool. As soon as he finds one he goes back to the fish and explains what he's about to do. To his surprise, it lets him lift it out of the water and carry it to the bigger pool, as if it understood every word. "You should be all right here until high tide," Rupert says as the fish circles the pool. He gets the odd impression that the fish gives him a grateful glance. "I suppose you were washed up by the squall," he goes on. Even though it seems as if the fish understands him, Rupert nearly jumps out of his skin when it pokes its head out of the water and starts to speak. "It's all my own fault. I should have known to stay away!"

RUPERT RESCUES THE FISH

*"King Neptune's cross and warned that he
Would stop boats putting out to sea!"*

*"The tide will soon come in again,
Perhaps you'd watch and tell me when?"*

*The fish leaps up and says, "The sea
Is nearer now, please carry me."*

*He cries "Thanks!" as they reach the shore
Then dives into the sea once more.*

Rupert is still staring in amazement as the fish goes on: "I knew all fish had been warned to stay away from Cocklesands Bay because it was the target of our King Neptune's wrath. I wasn't told why, so I thought I'd come and take a look at the place. Should have known better! That squall was a bit of Neptune's wrath, all right! By the way, has the tide started to come in yet?" "It . . . it's coming in fast," stammers Rupert, still astonished to meet a talking fish! At this, the fish leaps out of the water and casts a glance at the incoming tide. "It's close enough for you to carry me back now," it says. "Just hold out your arms." Rupert does as he is asked. The fish jumps up into his outstretched arms and Rupert hurries towards the water's edge. "Before you go, tell me how it is you can talk," he asks the fish. "Learned how to from Sea Sprites and the like," it replies proudly. "Thanks for saving me!" it cries, and, with a final flick of its tail, it dives into the sea.

RUPERT TELLS THE FISH'S TALE

Rupert runs back to tell his tale
And why the fishing's bound to fail.

"A talking fish!" cries Jem. "Flimflam!"
"No, Rupert never fibs," says Sam.

But why is Neptune cross with them?
"Perhaps he's lost something?" says Jem.

They all decide that must be why,
Then Jonty Jinks goes walking by.

Rupert races back to tell Jem and Sam about the fish and what he has learned from it – that the squalls are a sign of King Neptune's anger with Cocklesands. It's plain that Jem doesn't believe a word of his story. At least, he doesn't until Sam says, "It may sound far-fetched, Jem, but I've known Rupert a long time and 'pon my word, he never tells fibs. If he says it happened, then it did. Besides, when I was at sea I heard tales of Neptune's wrath – and of talking fish too."

"But why should Neptune be angry with Cocklesands?" cries Jem. "Perhaps someone has taken something valuable from the sea," suggests Sam. "He's got lots of precious things hidden away beneath the waves." But who in Cocklesands could have taken something valuable belonging to King Neptune? Rupert and the others are asking themselves this very question when Jonty Jinks comes strolling by. All at once, they find themselves thinking the same thing . . .

RUPERT SEES JINKS CHALLENGED

*"Jinks's new wealth!" cries Sam. "Could he
Have taken something from the sea?"*

*"Come back!" cries Jem. "Before you go,
There's something that I'd like to know . . ."*

*"This money that you say you're due –
You've found some treasure, haven't you!"*

*Jem's sure he's right, but Jinks won't say
He simply turns and walks away . . .*

"Jinks's new-found wealth!" cries Sam. "The money he says he's coming into soon! He was very mysterious about it when he spoke to young Rupert here." "Let's go and ask him about it, right now!" says Jem. "I don't suppose for a moment that he'll tell the truth, but its worth a try, to find out what he's been up to!" He hurries out of the cottage and calls to Jinks. "Wait a minute, Jonty. We want a word with you . . ." Jinks spins round, guiltily. He looks startled, then gives a sickly grin as Jem and Sam draw near. "This money you say you've got coming to you – the windfall that will let you give up fishing – you've taken something precious from the sea, haven't you?" demands Jem. Jink's jaw drops in dismay but he soon recovers and gives Jem a defiant stare. "'Tain't none of your business!" he blusters. "Nor anyone else in Cocklesands." With that he turns away sharply and scuttles up a flight of steps . . .

RUPERT OVERHEARS A CALL

"I wonder what the truth can be?"
Says Jem. "Oh dear, we're out of tea!"

He asks Rupert to buy some more
And sends him to the village store.

Rupert stops suddenly and blinks,
For by the 'phone stands Jonty Jinks!

"See you tonight!" he hears him say
As Jinks hangs up and goes to pay.

"Let's talk about this over a cup of tea," says Jem and leads the way back to his cottage. When they get there, Sam is just starting to say that he's sure Jinks *has* taken something valuable from the sea when Jem discovers that the tea caddy is empty. "I'll go and fetch some more," offers Rupert. Jem gives him the money and follows him outside to point the way. "The shop's just up this lane," he says. "Keep going and you can't miss it. It's our post office too."

Cocklesands post office has the only telephone in the village. When Rupert arrives at the post office he sees that someone's using it – Jonty Jinks! He is just in time to hear Jinks say, "Right then, you'll collect it tonight," before he hangs up. "He'll be coming out in a moment," thinks Rupert and looks around for a place to hide. As Jinks goes to pay, Rupert hears the postmistress say, "That was a Milchester number you rang, so it only counts as a local call . . ."

15

RUPERT FINDS A 'PHONE NUMBER

Jinks leaves and Rupert wonders who
It was he heard him talking to?

Inside the shop, he's quick to find
Some paper that Jinks left behind.

Rupert unfolds the screwed-up note
And reads a number that Jinks wrote.

"Someone in Milchester, you say?"
Cries Sam, "Let's call them right away!"

Rupert hides behind a post-box as Jinks comes out of the shop and hurries away. He wonders if he should follow him, in the hope of learning more, then he remembers the tea he's been sent to buy and enters the shop instead. "Some people have no idea of tidiness!" complains the postmistress. "The man who just left simply threw that piece of paper on the floor!" Rupert scoops up the ball of paper she points to. "Don't worry, I'll get rid of it for you," he says.

Before the postmistress can say another word, Rupert asks her for the packet of tea. As soon as he gets outside he unfolds the screwed up piece of paper and finds what looks like a telephone number written on it. He hurries back to the others straightaway. "You say he was calling Milchester?" says Sam when Rupert tells him everything that happened. "Well, it's pretty clear that this is the number he was calling. Let's ring it right now and find out whose it is."

RUPERT'S FRIEND MAKES A CALL

Sam asks to use the 'phone and then
Calls the same number once again . . .

He soon rings off and quickly goes
To tell the others what he knows.

"Who was it?" Jem asks anxiously.
A man Sam's heard of – Sir Humphrey!

"The man that Jinks was talking to
Is famous for his private zoo!"

"The postmistress will find it odd if Rupert goes back to the shop so soon," Sam tells Jem. "You two stay here, while I go inside and make the call." "What a coincidence! You're the second person to ask for that number today," says the postmistress. "I'll just put you through." Sam looks grim as he hears the person who answers the 'phone. "Sorry, wrong number!" he says and hangs up quickly. "Who was it?" ask Rupert and Jem anxiously.

"Sir Humphrey Pumphrey!" exclaims Sam. "I've heard lots about him in my time, and none of it very good!" As the friends make their way back to Jem's cottage, Sam explains that Sir Humphrey is the owner of a private zoo, which only he is ever allowed to see. "'Tis said it contains very rare creatures, for which he has paid a lot of money! People bring him animals they've caught from all over the world – he's none too worried how they're come by!"

17

RUPERT JOINS A NIGHT WATCH

Back at Jem's cottage, all agree
He must want something from the sea!

"We've got to stop him if we can!"
Says Jem. "Wait here, I've got a plan!"

When Jem returns he says that they
Must go to Jinks's straightaway . . .

"He's meeting someone here tonight.
We'll watch but keep well out of sight."

Over a meal that evening, the friends all agree it must be a living thing that Jinks has taken from the sea if Sir Humphrey Pumphrey wants it. "And he's collecting it tonight," says Rupert. "That's what Jinks said on the 'phone." "Then we'll keep watch on Jinks's place as soon as it's dark," declares Jem. "But what can we do?" Rupert asks. "Leave that to me," says Jem. "I've got an idea!" Telling the others he'll be back later, he gets up and makes for the door.

It is dark when Jem returns. He apologises for having been gone so long, but says there's no time to explain. "We've got to get up to Jinks's place straightaway!" he says. "Be sure to wrap up warm. We may have a long, cold wait." A few minutes later the three of them set off towards Jonty Jinks's home, warmly clad and carrying a couple of powerful torches. The cottage lies some distance from the village and as they draw near they can see a bright light shining in the window.

RUPERT SEES JINKS AMBUSHED

"Hush!" whispers Jem. "Don't breathe a word!"
As an approaching car is heard.

A fat man knocks at Jinks's door –
Sir Humphrey Pumphrey! Sam is sure . . .

Jinks carries something to the car.
"This way," says Pumphrey. "It's not far!"

"Stay there!" Sam cries out suddenly.
"You've stolen something from the sea!"

Jem leads the way to a clump of bushes from which they can watch Jinks's cottage without being seen. For a long time nothing happens, but Rupert is sure he can hear something moving When he mentions it Jem says it's nothing and tells him to hush. At last a car comes into sight. It pulls up outside the cottage and a large man gets out. He marches up to the front door, which is opened by Jinks. "Come in, Sir Humphrey," he greets his visitor. "It's in the bath-tub."

Sir Humphrey disappears inside, but soon emerges, together with Jinks, who is carrying something wrapped in a blanket. "Quickly, let's get this to my place," growls Sir Humphrey. "Now!" Jem cries as the chums step out from hiding and shine torches at the two men. "Whatever you have there is going straight back into the sea, where it belongs!" snaps Sam. Jinks and Sir Humphrey are too startled to speak, but from the mysterious bundle comes what sounds like a stifled sob . . .

RUPERT LEARNS JINKS'S SECRET

"Out of my way, and make it quick!"
Sir Humphrey cries and waves his stick.

Jem whistles loud and at the sound
His fishermen friends gather round.

"They're everywhere!" Sir Humphrey blinks.
Sam takes the strange bundle from Jinks . . .

He can't believe what meets his eyes!
"A little merboy!" Rupert cries.

Sir Humphrey is the first to recover. "Don't know who you are," he snarls, "but that bundle is going to my home. Out of my way." He raises his heavy stick. Sam steps in front of Rupert, as Jem gives a shrill whistle. Next moment, Sir Humphrey and Jinks find themselves surrounded by a crowd of grim-faced fishermen, who suddenly emerge from hiding places all around the cottage. Nobody speaks as they move forward and start to close in on the wretched pair.

Now Rupert sees what Jem was up to when he went off on his own. He must have spent all afternoon arranging the ambush! Sir Humphrey looks all round, then lowers his stick. Without a word Sam takes the bundle from Jinks, lays it gently down and undoes the belt which holds the blanket in place. As the blanket is unfolded a great gasp goes up from everyone except the two rogues. "Who'd have believed it!" Sam marvels. "A merboy!" cries Rupert.

RUPERT COMFORTS THE MERBOY

"You'll soon be safe, back in the sea,"
Says Rupert, reassuringly.

"I meant no harm!" Jinks starts to say.
"He got caught in my nets one day!"

Jem stops him with an angry stare.
"Leave Cocklesands!" he tells the pair.

"Thank you!" the Merboy says, "but now
I must get to the sea somehow . . ."

The merboy sits up and looks fearfully about him. "You're safe now," Rupert smiles. "You'll soon be back in the sea." "No wonder Neptune was so angry with us," breathes Sam. "He thought *we'd* stolen this merboy of his." The fishermen glare sternly at Sir Humphrey and the wretched Jinks. "I meant no harm," Jinks whines. "He got caught up in my nets and I couldn't resist the chance to make my fortune by selling him to a wealthy collector."

Rupert has never seen anyone look a stern as the fishermen do when they hear Jinks's tale. It is Jem who speaks for them all. "Leave Cocklesands at once!" he orders the crestfallen pair. "You can come back to collect your things," he tells Jinks. "But you, Sir Humphrey Pumphrey, don't come near here again!" The rogues look sheepish, then turn and scuttle away. "Thank you everyone," says a small voice. It is the Merboy speaking. "Now please put me back into the sea."

RUPERT SEES CALM SEAS RETURN

As Jem's boat nears the open sea
The Merboy dives in happily.

"Please give my thanks to everyone,
And Neptune's too, for what you've done!"

Next day the men watch nervously
As the first boat puts out to sea . . .

But soon they start to wave and cheer:
Neptune's forgiven them, it's clear.

They carry the merboy to Jem's boat and in next to no time the little craft is heading out across the bay. Jem explains that he daren't leave the bay for fear of Neptune's wrath. He asks the merboy to believe that no one in Cocklesands knew what Jinks was up to and reminds him of the part the local fishermen have played in his rescue. Before the merboy swims away he vows to tell Neptune that, far from being angry, he should be grateful to everyone in Cocklesands.

Next morning the whole village gathers to watch the first fishing boat put to sea. Rupert holds his breath as it reaches the edge of the bay but the sea remains calm and the breeze gentle. The men in the boat turn and wave happily as on it goes, further out to sea. The villagers give a rousing cheer and throw their hats into the air for joy. "Hooray!" laughs Rupert. "The merboy's kept his promise. Neptune's forgiven Cocklesands and everything's fine again." The End.

RUPERT
and the
Scared Crows

John Harrold.

RUPERT WAKES UP LATE

It's time to get up, but instead
Rupert is still asleep in bed.

He blinks his eyes and sits up straight,
Amazed to find he's slept so late!

"That's odd!" he thinks. "Most days I wake
Because of the noise the crows make."

"Today there's nothing to be heard.
And look! There's not a single bird!"

"Wake up, sleepy head!" Mrs. Bear shakes Rupert gently. Usually by this time he is up and starting to get ready. This morning, though, he is still sound asleep. At the sound of his mother's voice he stirs, then blinks and sits up with a start. "What time is it?" he asks. "Past your usual getting-up time," Mrs. Bear smiles. "Are you feeling all right?" "Yes, thanks," replies Rupert. "That's strange! Why didn't I wake up as usual this morning?"

At breakfast he is still puzzling over why he didn't wake up as usual. "It's rather as if something that happens each morning didn't today – something so usual that we just don't notice." He eats on still puzzling. Suddenly – "Crows!" he cries. "That's it! Their cawing wakes me each day. But they haven't cawed at all this morning." He dashes into the garden and looks towards the trees where the crows nest. There is no sign of them. Why?

RUPERT ASKS THE OWL TO HELP

Rupert sets out to find the crows
And meets the Wise Owl as he goes . . .

He tells him what's wrong, then suggests
The owl should look into their nests.

"Of course!" he hoots. "Wait here for me,"
And soars up to a nearby tree.

Then back he flies. "They're there all right,
But hiding, for they've all turned white!"

If there's one thing Rupert can't resist it's a mystery. So after breakfast he sets out to solve the riddle of the silent crows. On his way to their trees he sees the Wise Owl and asks him if he knows why the crows are so silent this morning. The Owl is mystified too. "Their cawing may wake you up but it lulls me to sleep after a hard night's flying and here I am still wide awake," he says. "What can be wrong?" "Why not fly up and have a look?" suggests Rupert. "Good idea," agrees the Owl and flaps away to inspect the crows' nests. For what seems a long time the Owl hovers over the big rough nests then turns and swoops back to where Rupert is waiting. It looks as shocked as an owl can look. "Well?" Rupert asks. "Well!" the Owl says after a long moment. "So far as I could see the crows are all there. But they are huddled in their nests, as though they're hiding. And stranger still – their feathers have all turned white!"

RUPERT QUESTIONS ODMEDOD

*"How strange," says Rupert. "Can it be
That something's scared them terribly?"*

*He thanks the owl, then says he'll go
To ask a friend who ought to know . . .*

*The scarecrow, Odmedod, can he
Have frightened the crows recently?*

*"Me, frighten crows?" he gasps. "Why you
Know that's the last thing I would do!"*

"White?" repeats Rupert, unable to believe his ears. The Owl nods. "True as I'm sitting here," he says. "And they look so scared! I've heard of folk's hair turning white with fright. But what can have scared the crows so badly?" "I can't imagine," replies Rupert. "But I'm going to try and find out!" "How?" the Owls asks. "Who better to ask about scared crows than a scarecrow?" says Rupert. And off he goes leaving the Owl looking very puzzled.

Few people in Nutwood know that Rupert can talk to scarecrows – well, one scarecrow, at any rate, one named Odmedod. And it's to this strange creature he hurries. He finds him in a field, looking pretty much like any other scarecrow. Rupert approaches the raggedy figure and demands, "Have you been scaring the crows near my house, Odmedod?" The scarecrow stares. "Scaring crows?" it repeats. "That's the last thing a scarecrow would do!"

RUPERT LEARNS OF A "MONSTER"

"We're friends, you see. The crows like me.
They know I stand here harmlessly."

A little bird swoops down. "I know
What terrified the poor crows so . . ."

"A monster flew up to their tree!
At least, that's what they all told me!"

Rupert decides to find out more.
"I'll ask the chief crow what he saw."

"It's a secret," Odmedod goes on. "You see, the birds aren't scared of us scarecrows. They know *we* can't harm them." "Then why don't they eat more of the farmers' seeds and crops?" asks Rupert. "Because," Odmedod replies, "if they did the farmers would see scarecrows are no good and use something *really* frightening in our place." Just then a little bird who has been listening pipes up, "I know what did scare the crows – a horrible monster!"

"A m – monster!" Rupert gasps. "What sort of monster?" "I don't know," says the bird. "I only know what the crows told me and all they'd say was, 'Ugh, the monster!'" "I'm going to take a look for myself," decides Rupert. Odmedod begs him to be careful. "It's all right," Rupert says. "I'm a good tree-climber." And he starts towards the crows' trees. "Try the nest in the tallest tree first," the bird calls to him. "It's the home of the chief crow."

RUPERT HEARS THE CROWS' TALE

"That must be his nest I can see
At the top of the tallest tree."

The chief crow sits there, looking glum,
Till Rupert tells him why he's come.

"We only saw the monster's head –
It snarled and filled us all with dread!"

The crow squawks with alarm and then
Cries out, "Oh no! It's back again!"

The clump of trees is still when Rupert gets there. Not a caw. Not a crow to be seen. He finds the tallest tree where he has been told the chief crow nests and starts to climb it carefully. He pauses when he gets near the nest. "I mustn't frighten the poor crow," he says to himself. "Hello," he calls softly. "It's only me – Rupert Bear. I've come to see if I can help." He climbs up and peers into the nest. There, sits a large, glum, white crow.

"I heard about the monster and I've come to see if there's anything I can do," Rupert goes on. "It must have been awful." "Worse than awful," croaks the crow. "A terrifying great face, looming over the trees, it was, and snarling at us. We were so scared – well, just look!" And it waves a wing at the other nests full of cringing white crows. Then the chief crow stares over Rupert's shoulder, opens its beak and screeches, "It's back!"

28

RUPERT SEES THE "MONSTER"

Rupert swings round and finds it's true,
For now he sees the monster too!

He's frightened too, until he sees
The "monster" flutter in the breeze . . .

"There's more to this than meets the eye!"
He thinks and bids the crow goodbye.

Then Rupert finds that he can hear
Somebody laughing somewhere near.

Rupert turns to meet a sight that all but topples him from his perch on the branch. A huge, fearsome face looms over the nests, teeth bared in a terrible snarl. "No wonder the crows turned white!" Rupert gasps. The face doesn't do anything – just hangs there looking terrifying. Then as he clings to the branch Rupert sees the face ripple in the breeze and press back against some sort of frame. "I know what that is!" he breathes to himself.

Now he's sure he knows what the monster is, Rupert decides to find out who's behind it. The crows are cowering in their nests, their eyes shut tight, not daring to look at the face. "I'll be back!" Rupert calls and shins down the tree as fast as he can. As soon as he reaches the ground, he starts running towards the side of the clump of trees where the face seemed to rise. He is almost at the edge of the trees when he hears a laugh. It's a laugh he knows well.

RUPERT TRACES THE "MONSTER"

Just as he thought! His guess was right!
The "monster" is a Chinese kite!

"Stop!" Rupert calls out to Ting-Ling
"Bring down the kite. Wind in the string!"

He tells his pals the way their kite
Has given all the crows a fright.

"Imagine how the crows will feel –
Their 'monster' wasn't even real!"

"As I thought!" cries Rupert as he bursts out of the trees. The laughter he heard was his friend Tigerlily's. She is the daughter of the Chinese Conjurer who lives in a pagoda near Nutwood. With her is a boy Rupert has met before, a friend Ting-Ling, who's here on a visit from China. They spot Rupert and Tigerlily calls, "Come and play!" "No!" Rupert cries. "Pull down that kite at once!" Ting-Ling is puzzled but he winds in the kite string.

The Chinese pair are upset to hear how they have scared the crows. "We should have thought!" says Tigerlily. "You see, it is an ancient war kite used for scaring enemies. Ting-Ling brought it to show me. We must tell the crows it is only a kite." "No!" Rupert says. "They're ashamed enough at being scared. They'll be even more so at being scared by just a kite. They'll never get their self-respect back. We have to think of something else."

RUPERT HATCHES A PLAN

*"We have to find a way to save
Their pride and show they're really brave!"*

*Then Rupert says, "It's up to you,
Ting-Ling. Here's what I want to do . . ."*

*As soon as he's explained his plan,
He runs as quickly as he can . . .*

*He starts to climb and doesn't stop
Until he's reached the very top.*

Somehow, Rupert tells the others, the crows must be made to feel brave again. And he urges them to think hard about how this can be done. As he thinks Rupert walks round the kite, studying it. Then – "Got it!" he cries. "Ting-Ling, you're good at flying a kite. Could you, for instance . . . ?" And he explains what he wants. "Easy!" chuckles the Chinese boy. "That's great!" Rupert says. "So here's what we're going to do –."

Rupert asks the others to give him time to get back to the chief crow's nest and a few minutes more before doing what they've planned. Then he hurries back through the trees. As he goes he thinks, "It's such a pity about those poor crows turning white. But if my plan works then at least they should feel better being brave white crows than cowardly white ones." And with that thought he starts to climb back up the tree towards the chief crow's nest.

RUPERT PUTS HIS PLAN TO WORK

*"The monster looked Chinese and so
I went to see some friends I know . . ."*

*"I asked them for advice and they
Said noise would frighten it away!"*

*The chief crow smiles. "Well if you're sure
Then all we have to do is caw!"*

*He turns and tells the others how
They'll scare away the monster now . . .*

"Now you know how awful the monster is," the chief crow greets Rupert. "Even you ran away." "Not really ran away," Rupert says. "It looked Chinese and since I have two Chinese friends nearby I went to ask them about it." "And?" asks the crow. "And when I described it," goes on Rupert, "they said, yes, it is Chinese and does look very frightening. But they told me something else about it. It is absolutely terrified of loud noise!"

"Do you mean it would run away if we made a lot of noise?" asks the chief crow. "Well, my friends say it would," Rupert replies. The chief crow is silent for a moment then hops onto the edge of its nest and croaks loudly. The other crows which have been cowering in their nests turn towards it. As the chief addresses them in crow language they perk up and by the time the chief has finished they are cawing excitedly from nest to nest.

RUPERT'S PLAN SUCCEEDS

"It's back!" the chief crow cries in awe.
"Come on!" calls Rupert. "Start to caw!"

The chief starts, then they all join in –
They've never made a louder din!

They flap their wings until they see
The monster tremble timidly . . .

And now it's clear the crows have made
The monster scared – it looks dismayed.

"Any time now, Ting-Ling," Rupert breathes. And as if Ting-Ling has heard, over the trees rises "the monster". For a moment the crows are shocked into silence. Their perkiness vanishes. It looks as if, after all, the awful face is too much for them. Then Rupert acts. "CAW!" he shouts as loudly as he can. There is an instant's silence. Then "Caw!" croaks the chief crow loudly. And every single crow rises and joins in the defiant din.

In all the time he has lived near their trees Rupert has never known the crows make so much noise, nor sound so angry. For a long moment the great face looms over them, teeth bared, tongue sticking out in a frightful snarl. Suddenly it wobbles. It twists. It turns upside down. And the crows screech louder then ever. For the horrible snarl has disappeared, replaced by a look of fear and dismay. "Good flying, Ting-Ling!" Rupert breathes to himself.

33

RUPERT'S JOB IS DONE

Just one more caw and off it goes,
Defeated by the hero crows!

The crows all laugh delightedly –
They've won a famous victory . . .

The chief boasts, "Even though we're white,
We gave that monster quite a fright!"

"Well done!" cries Rupert. "I'm quite sure
He's left Nutwood for evermore!"

Before the crows can get too close a look at the new "frightened" face, it plunges out of sight – which is just what Rupert and Ting-Ling agreed should happen. "What a kite-flier!" Rupert thinks. He looks round at the crows. He is certain they've no idea the "monster" was only an old Chinese kite. As they hop up and down and caw it is quite plain that they believe they have won a famous victory – which is exactly what Rupert wants them all to think.

"I've never seen the like," Rupert tells the chief crow. "Yes, we *were* rather good," croaks the crow. "Did you see its face? Terrified of us, it was." "Yes, it certainly looked it," Rupert agrees. "But then crows *are* brave birds." The crow preens itself. "And we certainly were," it says. "Even though we are white." And so, satisfied that the crows have their self-respect back, Rupert says goodbye and climbs down from the tree.

RUPERT SEES BLACK CROWS BACK

"It worked!" laughs Rupert. "Did you hear?
The crows have overcome their fear!"

Ting-Ling and Tigerlily say
They'll keep the kite hidden away.

Next morning, Rupert's glad to wake
And hear the sound his crow friends make.

And, as they've got their courage back,
The Nutwood crows have all turned black . . .

Rupert runs to where Tigerlily and Ting-Ling are waiting. "It worked!" he laughs. "The crows believe they're really brave and aren't so bothered about being white. Ting-Ling's kite-flying did it." "But it was you who saw what the kite looked like upside-down," Ting-Ling says. "It's strange that we have never noticed it." As Rupert starts for home Tigerlily calls, "We shan't fly the kite again, just in case!" "Good thinking!" Rupert chuckles.

When Mrs. Bear enters Rupert's bedroom next morning he is awake and at the open window. "Listen to that!" he greets her. "The crows are back! Louder than ever . . ." Mrs. Bear joins him at the window. "But you said they'd all turned white!" she gasps. "Yes, they've got their real colour back," Rupert laughs. "I suppose if believing they were scared made them lose it then believing they're really brave after all must have brought it back." The End

RUPERT

Rupert and Bill are on their way
To start a boating holiday.

Rupert and Bill are off on a weekend boating trip, together with their pals, Algy Pug and Bingo, who have gone on ahead to set up camp. They are paddling along quietly, when the calm of the river is suddenly shattered by the roar of a speeding motor boat. The pals look back in alarm and gasp aloud at what they see. Bearing down on them is fast launch with two men in it! "Look out!" cries Bill. "They're coming straight at us!"

and the River Rogues

When suddenly the shocked pals find
A fast boat racing up behind . . .

They paddle hard and just get clear,
Although the boat's still very near.

The two pals paddle for all they're worth and manage to get out of the launch's way just in time. It speeds past, sending a huge wave over their little boat, which snatches the paddle from Rupert's grasp. But the men in the launch don't stop to help. Far from it. They turn and wave their fists as if the pals were to blame for the near miss. Then they race away, leaving the astonished chums floundering in their wake.

The motor boat goes racing past,
Then heads upstream, still travelling fast.

RUPERT'S PALS' TENT IS EMPTY

*"Gosh! That was close," gasps Bill. "Those men
Almost capsized our boat just then."*

*The pair press on until they see
The spot where their pals' camp must be.*

*Bingo and Algy are not there –
"They must have ventured off somewhere!"*

*The pals unpack and agree they
Should put their tent up straightaway.*

"Gosh! That was close" gasps Bill as the waves die down. He recovers the lost paddle and helps Rupert set the boat to rights. At last they finish bailing out the water they have shipped and are ready to set off again. After a while they reach the grassy bank where Algy and Bingo have pitched their tent. There is no sign of either of them. "I expect they're inside the tent," says Rupert. "And probably beginning to wonder what's kept us so long."

The pals pull in to the bank, tie up to a tree stump and scramble ashore. "We're here!" Rupert calls. But there's no answer. He peers into the tent. 'They're not here," he says. "Nor's their boat," adds Bill as he looks around. "They can't be far away, though. Come on, let's put our tent up before they come back." So the pals unroll their tent and are relieved to find that it's still dry inside, despite their earlier soaking from the speeding launch.

RUPERT SPIES A BACKWATER

Then, by the far bank, Rupert sees
Two swans glide out beneath the trees.

The willows hide something, he's sure,
So off they paddle, to explore . . .

The leaves part and they slowly glide
Towards what's on the other side.

An old boathouse comes into view –
Algy and Bingo's boat's there too!

Rupert and Bill settle down to wait for Algy and Bingo. On the far bank of the river there are some large willow trees, whose branches reach down to the water, like a curtain of green leaves. All of a sudden the branches part and out glide two swans. "Look, Bill!" calls Rupert. "There's a hidden backwater. I bet that's where the others have gone. Come on, let's go and see!" Next moment, the pair have climbed back into their boat and are paddling slowly across the river.

The boat glides gently through the curtain of leaves and the pals suddenly find themselves paddling along a hidden stretch of river. It is very still and green and looks as if it's hardly ever used. Some way along it stands an old boathouse, which has a small boat tied up beside it. "That's Algy and Bingo's boat!" says Bill. "You were right, Rupert. They're here somewhere. They must have tied it up to the jetty and gone off to explore. Let's see if we can find them."

RUPERT FINDS THE LAUNCH

*"It's clear the others must have found
This place and gone to look around."*

*"We'll tie our boat securely here
And see if they are somewhere near . . ."*

*Inside the boathouse they soon find
A second boat's been left behind.*

*"The motor boat!" gasps Bill. "Oh no!
If it's here then we'd better go!"*

"Why should anyone have a boat-house hidden away in a quiet place like this?" wonders Rupert as they paddle closer. He sees why when they reach it and find an overgrown garden that stretches back to a big, old house. "What a place!" cries Bill. "It doesn't look as though anyone's lived here for ages. Let's go and see if Algy and Bingo have gone off to have a look around." "Good idea!" agrees Rupert and ties the boat up securely to the boat-house.

The two pals scramble on to the shaky landing-stage of the boat-house and peer through a grimy window. Rupert gasps in surprise at what they see inside – a newish-looking motor-launch! "I'm sure that's the one that nearly ran us down!" he exclaims. "You're right!" whispers Bill. "I don't like the look of this. I think we should get out of here as fast as we can . . ." "But what about Bingo and Algy?" replies Rupert. "We can't just go without making sure they're all right."

RUPERT RECOGNISES A MAN

"No!" Rupert says. "Before we do,
We've got to find the other two."

The pals crawl on their hands and knees,
Then, suddenly, Bill starts to sneeze!

A man peers out but doesn't see
The pair, who crouch down anxiously.

"It is the same men and it's clear
They're up to no good, hiding here!"

As their launch is moored in the boat-house, it seems pretty certain that the men the pals saw earlier are lurking somewhere nearby. Even so, Bill agrees with Rupert that they must make sure their pals aren't in any sort of trouble. They start off towards the house, crawling on their hands and knees. With only a few yards to go, Bill whispers urgently, "This grass is tickling my nose!" "Oh no!" groans Rupert as his friend gives a deafening sneeze . . .

The pals freeze anxiously as a window is flung open and a cross-looking man looks out. He peers all around for a long time, then shrugs and shuts the window. "Did you see who that was?" whispers Rupert. "No," says Bill, "I was too busy trying not to sneeze again!" "Well, we were right about the launch in the boat-house," says Rupert. "He was one of the men who almost ran us down! I don't like this, Bill. I'm sure the pair of them are up to no good."

The pair creep closer until they
Can hear each word the two men say . . .

The crooks have caught their friends – what now?
"We've got to rescue them somehow!"

"There's only one thing for it, we
Must find a way in secretly."

"The back door's closed, but, even so
It may give way, you never know . . ."

The pals feel far from brave but, having come so far, they're not going to give up before finding out what's going on. The man who looked out has not shut the window completely and they creep up to it as quietly as they can. When they get nearer they can hear a man talking. "Once we've sorted out the loot from that last job we'll be off." "What about those two upstairs?" a second man asks. "We'll deal with them later," comes the ominous reply. "Algy and Bingo!" gasps Rupert.

Rupert beckons Bill to follow and leads the way round the corner of the house so that they can discuss what to do next. Somehow, they decide, their pals must be rescued before the two men are ready to leave. "They seem busy enough for the moment," Rupert says. "Let's see if we can find an unlocked door and get inside without them hearing." Sure enough, when they steal round to the back of the house they find a door that looks promising. But is it unlocked?

RUPERT IS TRAPPED

*At first the door won't move, but then
It opens as they push again.*

*Upstairs the pals try to decide
Which room their chums must be inside.*

*The door's locked but it's Algy who
Replies, "Rupert, can it be you?"*

*Just then a cry comes from the stairs:
A man has caught them unawares!*

The pals are in luck! To their delight, they find that the door *is* unlocked but they have to push really hard before it will open. Just inside the door there is a staircase. "Come on!" whispers Rupert. The pair creep up the stairs, which seem to creak alarmingly at every step. At the top they are faced by three or four closed doors. "We know they're upstairs, so they must be in one of these rooms," whispers Rupert. "Let's try this one first." He points to the nearest door.

Cautiously, he turns the handle and pushes, but the door doesn't open. He stoops to the keyhole and hisses, "Algy, Bingo, are your there?" "Rupert!" comes Algy's excited voice. "We're locked in. Can you get us out?" "There's no key on this side," Rupert whispers back. "The men downstairs . . ." But his words are cut short by a sudden cry of rage. The men must have heard the pals after all, for one of them is advancing towards them up the stairs . . .

RUPERT LEARNS WHAT HAPPENED

"More snoopers, eh? My mate was sure
He heard a noise – now that makes four!"

He grabs the pals, then angrily
Shoves them inside and turns the key.

"Those men are crooks!" Bingo explains.
"They're counting their ill-gotten gains!"

"We overheard their plans but they
Caught us before we got away!"

Rupert and Bill look around desperately for somewhere to escape, but soon realise that they're trapped. The man towers over them angrily. "More of you, eh?" he snarls. "Well it's about time you learnt that it doesn't pay to meddle with me and my mate." He produces a key from his pocket and unlocks the door. Then he bundles them into the room with a cry of, "This will keep you out of the way. You can stay here with your chums until we're ready to leave!"

The door slams shut and Rupert asks Bingo if he knows what the men are up to. "We've stumbled on a thieves' den," says Bingo glumly. It turns out that he and Algy found the house when they decided to explore the backwater. At first it seemed deserted, but as they passed a window they heard the two men discussing their loot. "We tried to slip away," he adds. "But they spotted us and locked us up in here. Now it seems we're all in the same boat!"

RUPERT PLANS AN ESCAPE

"They'll leave as soon as morning dawns
With all their booty!" Algy warns . . .

He sighs and points, "If only we
Could reach the skylight and climb free."

"Let's try to move that big crate so
It's in position, right below . . ."

They push with all their strength and weight
And slowly start to move the crate.

"How long do you think they'll keep us here?" asks Bill. "No idea," Algy replies. "But they're planning on leaving pretty soon. We heard them say they'll set off at first light tomorrow, together with all their loot." "Early tomorrow!" breathes Bill. "I wonder if they'll take us with them or just leave us locked up here?" "I don't know," says Rupert. "But we've got to get out of here as soon as we can!" "We've already tried," sighs Algy, pointing up at a skylight. "We thought of getting out on to the roof," explains Bingo. "There might be a fire-escape we could climb down. The only way we could reach the skylight is by moving that big crate underneath it and climbing up. The trouble is, it's far too heavy to move!" "Perhaps the four of us might be able to shift it together," says Rupert. "Let's have another try." The four pals push against the crate with all their might. At first nothing happens. Then it starts to slide slowly forgward.

RUPERT'S PALS GO FOR HELP

Then, climbing up, Rupert finds he
Can reach the window easily.

"This way," he whispers. "Look! I've found
A ladder leading to the ground."

The ladder's old but seems to be
Safe as they climb down carefully.

While two pals stay, the others go
To tell the police all they know.

At last the crate is in position directly under the skylight. The pals scramble up on to it as Rupert prises open the skylight and props it up so that they can all climb out. It's dark outside but by the light of the moon they can see there is a parapet running along the edge of the roof. What's more, only a few feet away from them is an iron ladder which reaches to the ground. "That's a bit of luck," declares Rupert. "Just what we need to get away without raising the alarm."

The house may be old and run-down but the ladder seems pretty sturdy. Telling the others to take care, Rupert leads the way down, testing each rung before he trusts it with his whole weight. As soon as they reach the ground the pals put a safe distance between themselves and the house, before discussing what to do next. The best thing, they decide, is for Algy and Bingo to go off in their boat to fetch the police, while Rupert and Bill stay behind and keep watch.

*"Their boat!" gasps Rupert. "What if they
Leave before dawn and get away?"*

*"While they're asleep, let's go and see
The boathouse. Quick, Bill! Follow me . . ."*

*The motor boat's still there but how
Can the chums stop it leaving now?*

*"I know!" cries Bill. "This spare rope here
Has given me a good idea . . ."*

As Algy and Bingo hurry away, Rupert and Bill take up position behind a bush. The house is silent and still. "With a bit of luck, they'll both be asleep!" says Bill. "If they're leaving at first light they'll have gone to bed early." A sudden thought strikes Rupert. "What if they decide to leave before the others get back?" he whispers. He thinks hard then says, "Let's go and have another look at their boat. There must be something we can do to stop them getting away."

The pair hurry down to the boat-house, where the crooks' launch is still safely moored. It is the sight of the boat's mooring line that gives Bill an idea. He smiles and takes down a spare coil of rope. "If the boat was tied up with this, it would really slow them down," he tells Rupert. "And if we hid it out of sight it would take them simply ages to work out what had happened." "I think I see what you mean," says Rupert. "Come on," Bill urges, "Let's give it a try . . ."

RUPERT'S PLAN IS ALL SET

"Secure the boat," he tells his friend,
Then firmly knots the other end.

Then, making sure the boat's tied tight,
They hide the rope well out of sight.

As soon as it gets light they see
The two men leaving hurriedly.

Each man is carrying a bag
Which bulges full of stolen swag!

The pals carry the coil of rope to the back of the boat-house. Rupert ties one end to the stern of the launch, while Bill leans down and fastens the other to one of the posts on which the boat-house stands. They take care to leave plenty of slack so that most of the rope is hidden underwater. "We'll cover the rest of the rope with this old tarpaulin," says Rupert. "If they try to leave before it gets light I bet they won't see it at all. Well done, Bill! Now, let's get back."

The pals resume their watch on the house again. Nothing happens until it starts to get light, and Bill hisses, "They're leaving!" Rupert looks to where he's pointing and sees the two men come out of the house with bulging sacks over their shoulders. "That will be their loot!" he whispers. They manage to get near enough to hear one of the crooks growl, "Who'd have thought they would escape like that? The sooner we're away from here the better."

RUPERT'S PLAN WORKS TOO WELL

The pals stay hidden as the men
Head back towards their boat again.

An engine starts and before long
Their boat appears – Bill's plan's gone wrong!

But suddenly the flimsy shed
Starts shaking and the boat stops dead.

Next moment there's a crashing sound
And shattered timbers fall all round!

Rupert and Bill watch nervously as the two men carry their swag into the boat-house. "Those little perishers will have gone for the cops!" says one. "Let's get going." There is the sound of the men climbing into the launch and their loot being stowed away, then the boat's engine roars into life. The pals hold their breath and wait for cries of rage as the men find their boat won't move. To their dismay the engine gets louder and they see the launch start to nose out of the boat-house.

For a moment it looks as if pals' plan has come unstuck. Then the launch jerks to a sudden stop. The boat-house creaks and sways as the boat tugs at its hidden mooring line. Next moment it collapses on top of the two flabbergasted robbers in a jumble of splintered wood. The pals gasp as the launch vanishes in a great cloud of dust and shattered timber. "W..what have we done?" stammers Bill. "I certainly didn't expect anything like this to happen!"

RUPERT'S PALS BRING HELP

The boat has disappeared from sight
But are the two men still all right?

Their cabin kept them safe from harm.
"Quick, hide!" cries Rupert in alarm.

But then he sees a launch appear.
"We're safe now, the police are here!"

The crooks are still shocked as can be
And give themselves up harmlessly.

Aghast at the result of their plan, Rupert and Bill race to the ruins of the boat-house. As the dust settles they are relieved to find that the launch is not badly damaged after all. Although their boat is held fast by the tangle of wreckage, its cabin has saved the men from anything worse than a bad fright. Shaken and bewildered, the crooks gape at the remains of the boat-house in disbelief. "Let's get out of here before they spot us!" cries Rupert. But before the pals can move they hear the engine of a boat and turn to see a police launch pushing aside the curtain of willows that conceals the backwater. Algy and Bingo are aboard and the boat stops to let them ashore before moving up to where the crooks wait helplessly amid the wreckage. Excitedly, Bingo and Algy tell Rupert and Bill of their race to fetch the river police and how they were asked to guide them back to the deserted house while the police launch towed their rowing boat behind it.

RUPERT HEARS OF A REWARD

"Well done! We knew about these two
But only caught them thanks to you!"

"Once all these things have been restored
I think there might be a reward . . ."

The police launch sets off and then
The pals row to their camp again.

They find that staying up all night
Has given them an appetite!

Before they take the crooks away, one of the policemen comes to thank the pals. "We knew this pair were behind a spate of local robberies," he says. "Now, thanks to you, we know how they escaped with the loot and vanished after each job. I must say, we'd never have thought of looking for them in this deserted old backwater!" He opens one of the sacks and shows the pals some of the loot. "I should be surprised if there isn't a reward for helping to recover this," he grins.

Off goes the police launch, followed through the trailing willows by Rupert and the pals, who are all keen to get on with their camping trip. Food is their first thought when they reach their tents on the far side of the river and soon a panful of sausages is sizzling over the fire. "I've just had a thought!" says Rupert. "Seeing how long it is since we last had a meal, I'm not sure if this counts as a terribly late supper or an awfully early breakfast." The End

These two pictures of Mrs. Bear with a letter for Rupert look identical, but there are eleven differences between them. Can you spot them all? *(Answers on page 98)*

SPOT THE

DIFFERENCE

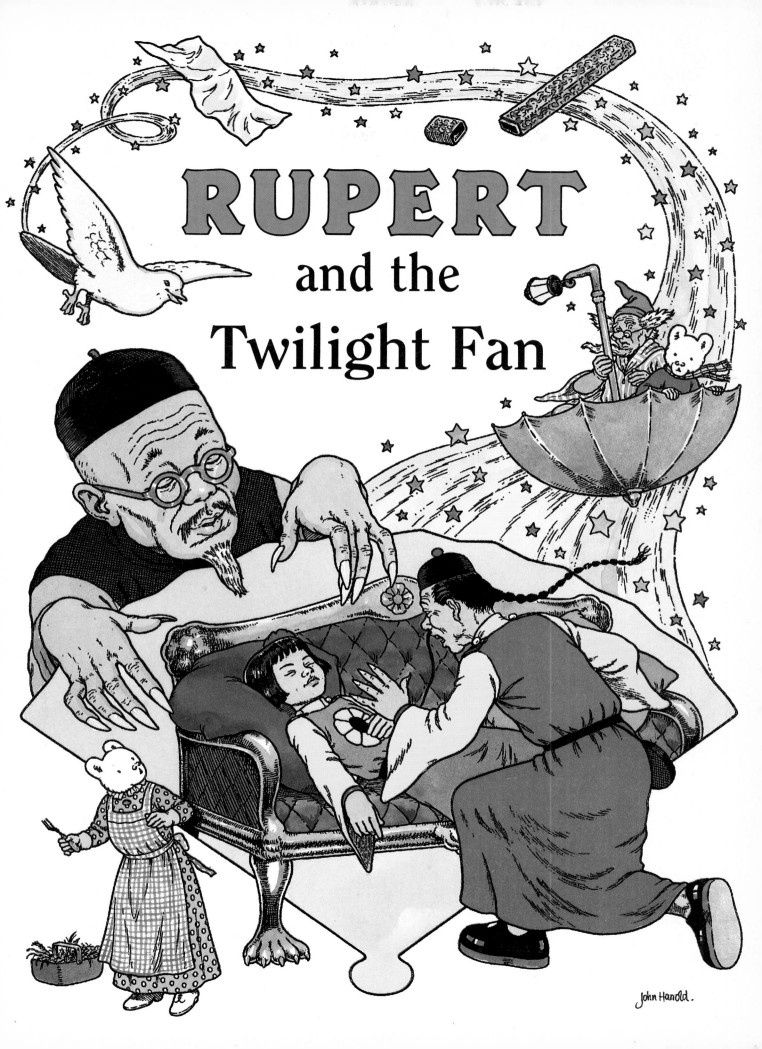

RUPERT
and the
Twilight Fan

John Harrold.

RUPERT IS INVITED TO LUNCH

To help his mum, Rupert agrees
To carry home the groceries.

On entering the shop the pair
See Tigerlily standing there.

"We have a guest," she starts to say.
"The Sage of Um has come to stay . . ."

"I'd love to see him!" Rupert cries.
"Then come to lunch," his friend replies.

One day Rupert's mother asks him to come with her to the village store. "I've got so many things to buy that I'll need some help to carry them all home," she explains. When they reach Mr. Chimp's shop, Rupert is delighted to find his friend, Tigerlily, doing some shopping for her father, the Chinese Conjurer. "I'm sorry to keep you waiting," she says, "but we've got a guest staying at the moment and I've lots of extra things to buy." "Who is it?" asks Rupert.

"The Sage of Um," Tigerlily replies. "He and my father like to meet every now and again to talk about their latest spells!" Rupert has met the Sage before, a jolly old man who lives on the island of Um, together with the last herd of unicorns in the world, and travels about in a strange flying craft, called the Brella. "I'd love to see him again!" he tells Tigerlily. "Then come to lunch tomorrow!" she declares. "May I?" Rupert asks his mother. "Of course!" she smiles.

RUPERT MEETS A STRANGER

Next day he sets off with a smile
And thinks of Um, the Sage's isle.

But on the way he has a fright
When someone grips his shoulder tight.

A Chinaman is standing there.
"Please don't be frightened, little bear . . ."

"There's something I'd like you to do
For me, and the Conjurer too."

Next day, Rupert sets off across Nutwood common towards the pagoda tower where Tigerlily and the Chinese Conjurer live. As he walks along he finds himself thinking about the Sage of Um's unicorns and how he once helped to save them from being captured by a wicked magician who wanted their horns for a special spell . . . He is still deep in thought when a mysterious figure suddenly steps out from behind a clump of bushes and grips him by the shoulder.

Rupert spins round to find an old man dressed in Chinese robes. "Please don't be frightened, little bear," he says. "I didn't mean to startle you." Pointing to the pagoda tower, the stranger asks Rupert if he knows the Conjurer who lives there. When he finds that Rupert is a friend of his daughter, he smiles and says, "How fortunate! I wonder if I can ask you to do something? It would be a great help to me and, I hope, to your friends as well . . ."

"I must explain that long ago
We used to be close friends, you know."

"One day we quarrelled, and since then
We vowed never to meet again!"

"But now I'd like to make amends
And see if we can still be friends."

"He might not see me, but if you
Speak to his daughter, that will do."

"The reason I have come to Nutwood is to put an end to an argument that took place many years ago," the stranger declares. "When the Conjurer and I were young we both lived at the Emperor's court where we studied magic together and became close friends. One day, we had a terrible quarrel and parted, vowing never to meet again. The Conjurer left China shortly afterwards and I haven't seen him since. Now I am older, I want to make amends before it is too late."

"But how can *I* help?" asks Rupert. The man looks thoughtful. "Mending an old quarrel is difficult," he says. "Even after all these years the Conjurer may still refuse to see me. If you could persuade his daughter to speak to him on my behalf, then I'm sure he will be more ready to listen . . ." "I don't suppose it will do any harm to ask her," agrees Rupert. "Oh, thank you!" cries the man. "Please be sure to offer her this as a token of my gratitude."

RUPERT AGREES TO HELP

*"Please give her this, but only when
You see her on her own again."*

*"If you can see her secretly,
I'll wait till she brings word to me."*

*"Hello!" says Tigerlily. "Come,
My father's with the Sage of Um."*

*Glad to have found her on her own,
Rupert asks, "Can we talk alone?"*

The Chinaman shows Rupert a beautifully carved box. "Please give her this when she is all alone," he asks. "The success of my mission depends on absolute secrecy until I know that her father has forgotten all about our old quarrel." Rupert is surprised at the stranger's request, but agrees to do as he's been asked. "Tell her it's a present from one who knew her father long ago," the old man urges Rupert. "I shall stay here by this signpost and await her reply . . ."

Hurrying on his way, so as not to be late for lunch, Rupert soon reaches the Conjurer's pagoda and knocks at the door. "Hello, Rupert!" cries Tigerlily. "I'm so glad you were able to come. My father and the Sage are both looking forward to seeing you." Keeping the stranger's present well out of sight, Rupert asks Tigerlily if he may talk to her alone for a few moments before they join the others. "Of course," she says, looking puzzled. "Follow me . . ."

RUPERT DELIVERS THE GIFT

*"Of course," she says, "but please tell me
What lies behind this mystery . . ."*

*"Your father's old friend sends this gift.
He hopes to end their ancient rift . . ."*

*She takes the box and finds the man
Has sent a lovely Chinese fan.*

*"Look!" Rupert says and reaches for
A note that's fallen to the floor.*

"We can talk in here without being overheard," Tigerlily tells Rupert. "But why are you acting so mysteriously all of a sudden?" "I've been asked to give you a secret message by someone your father used to know, many years ago," Rupert explains. Describing the Chinaman he's just met, he tells her how the stranger wants to patch up an old quarrel but daren't meet the Conjurer in case he hasn't been forgiven. "He hopes that you will speak for him and sends this present as a token of his gratitude."

"How exciting!" declares Tigerlily. "I wonder what it can be?" Taking the box from Rupert, she opens it to reveal a neatly-folded object tucked inside. "Why, it's a Chinese fan!" she cries and pulls it from its case. As she does so a small piece of paper flutters to the ground but Tigerlily is so delighted with the fan she doesn't seem to notice. "Look!" says Rupert and bends down to pick it up, just as Tigerlily waves the fan with a flourish.

RUPERT'S CHUM FALLS ASLEEP

He picks it up but hears a sound
Behind him as he turns around.

Is Tigerlily playing games?
"She's fast asleep!" Rupert exclaims . . .

"Help!" Rupert cries out anxiously.
"Something is wrong! Please come and see!"

The Conjurer hears Rupert's cries
And runs to where his daughter lies.

As Rupert leans forward to pick up the scrap of paper he hears Tigerlily give a deep sigh and drop the fan with a clatter. He spins round anxiously, only to see her lying on a low couch, looking exactly as if she had suddenly fallen asleep! There is a slight smile on Tigerlily's face and at first Rupert thinks she must be playing games. He tries to wake her but finds it's no use. Tigerlily isn't pretending, she really *is* fast asleep!

Unable to wake his friend, Rupert runs from the room and calls for help. His cries of alarm are answered by the Chinese Conjurer, who dashes from his study, closely followed by the Sage of Um. "It's Tigerlily!" Rupert gasps. "There's something wrong. She suddenly fell asleep and I just can't wake her . . ." With a cry of dismay, the Conjurer rushes past Rupert and heads straight for the couch. He stoops over his sleeping daughter and speaks to her gently. "Wake up, Tigerlily. Please, wake up . . ."

RUPERT'S FRIENDS ARE SHOCKED

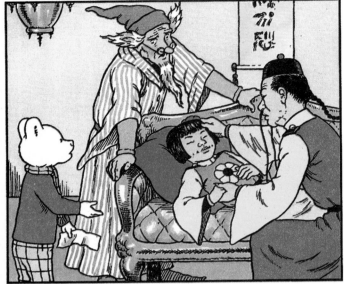

*He cannot wake her and grows pale
As Rupert starts to tell his tale . . .*

*"I think you were tricked by the man
You met, Rupert. Don't touch the fan!"*

*The message that the stranger wrote
Makes him gasp as he reads the note.*

*The Sage of Um reads on, "This man
Has sent – oh, no! – The Twilight Fan!"*

No matter how desperately the Conjurer tries to rouse his daughter, she slumbers on without showing any sign of waking. "Tell me everything that happened," he says to Rupert. "Be sure you leave out nothing!" He grows pale as Rupert describes the stranger he met and how he gave him a fan to take to Tigerlily as a secret gift. "Don't touch it!" he cries as Rupert bends down to pick up the fan. The man you met *meant* this to happen, Rupert. He tricked you into bringing the fan."

Poor Rupert is appalled to think that he's been tricked by the stranger! The Conjurer spots the scrap of paper he is holding and asks if it came with the fan. "Yes," says Rupert. He hands the note to the Conjurer, who peers at it closely, then starts to read aloud. "Please accept this token of my true feelings for your father. It is – oh, no!" The conjurer breaks off and hands the paper to the Sage. He kneels helplessly beside Tigerlily as the Sage reads on, "It is – the Twilight Fan!"

RUPERT IS TOLD ABOUT THE FAN

The Conjurer turns with a groan,
"Tung-tai's revenge, I might have known!"

The Sage of Um explains their fears:
The fan makes people sleep for years!

The Sage says he must go and look
For something in a special book.

"By looking here I hope to tell
If there's a way to break the spell . . ."

"I should have guessed!" groans the Conjurer. "This is Tung-tai's work. At last he has taken his terrible revenge!" Rupert looks puzzled until the Sage explains that it was Tung-tai he met on his way to the Conjurer's home. "It is true that they were both at the Emperor's court together many years ago," he tells Rupert. "But Tung-tai was dismissed for using wicked spells and the Conjurer became court magician in his place. Tung-tai swore revenge and now he has taken it!

"The fan he gave you was covered in a magic powder which sent Tigerlily to sleep. Unless the spell is broken, she could slumber on for years!" "Just like Sleeping Beauty!" gasps Rupert. "Exactly!" replies the Sage. He ponders for a moment, then asks the Conjurer if he may use his library. "Of course," he replies. Beckoning to Rupert, the Sage leads the way to the library and reaches down a heavy old book. "This is all about sleeping spells and potions," he declares.

RUPERT LEARNS ABOUT A CURE

"Yes!" reads the Sage, then looks forlorn.
"Tail feathers from the Dove of Dawn!"

"Perhaps the Bird King will agree
To help," says Rupert. "He knows me . . ."

"He has a palace in the air.
Your Brella could soon take us there!"

The Conjurer is told their plan
To help his daughter if they can.

The Sage pores over the old book for a long time. At last he turns to Rupert and says, "Yes, there is a way to break the spell of the Twilight Fan!" Then, as he reads on, he sighs and looks glum. "Tigerlily can only be woken if she is fanned using the tail feathers of the Dove of Dawn. Only one such bird exists, a treasured pet of the King of the Birds." "But I know the King!" cries Rupert. "I've met him before. We get on so well I'm sure he'll agree to help us if he can . . ." "The King may want to help," says the Sage, "but I don't think he'll agree to give up any feathers from his Dove of Dawn." "At least let's ask him!" Rupert pleads. "We can fly to his palace in your Brella!" "You're right!" declares the Sage and hurries to tell the Conjurer what's happening. "There is only a slim chance that we will be successful," he warns. "Please spare no effort!" the Conjurer cries. "A thousand thanks, my friends, may your journey be successful."

RUPERT AND THE SAGE SET OUT

The Sage makes sure he knows the way,
Then off they go, without delay."

Down towards Rupert's house they fly,
Then hover there to say goodbye.

"Take care!" says Mrs. Bear. "I'll see
You later, when it's time for tea!"

Then up into the air they go,
Till Nutwood's left far down below.

Rupert and the Sage run outside to where the Brella is waiting. They climb aboard and take off straightaway. The Sage produces a book and starts to leaf through it hurriedly. "Flight path from Nutwood to Bird Kingdom," he mutters. "Can we stop at my house on the way, so I can tell Mummy where I'm going?" asks Rupert. "Of course!" cries the Sage. "It will give me a chance to say hello again." A moment later the Brella is swooping down towards Mrs. Bear.

It doesn't land but hovers steadily above her as Rupert calls down to explain what's happened. "We can't stop!" he cries. "We're on our way to get something from the Bird King to try to break the spell . . ." "Well, do be careful!" says Mrs. Bear. "And drop in for a cup of tea as soon as you get back," she calls up to the Sage. "It will be so nice to see you again." Next minute, the Brella spins round and soars high into the air. In no time at all it has flown off, leaving Nutwood far behind.

Across the sky the Brella streaks –
High over trees and mountain peaks.

At last it slows and glides to rest
Where all the Bird King's subjects nest.

A court official's angered by
The way the Sage and Rupert fly!

"Arrest this pair!" he cries. "And bring
Them to be tried before the King!"

Rupert and the Sage remain deep in thought as the Brella races over wild highlands and up towards the Bird King's palace. Rupert soon recognises the palace in the clouds from which all birds are ruled. He has met the Bird King before and knows that he is friendly. He only hopes that the King likes him enough to listen to his story and agree to give up some feathers from the Dove of Dawn. "We'll soon find out!" says the Sage as the Brella starts to descend.

As the Brella lands in the palace courtyard, Rupert suddenly remembers how much the Bird King dislikes all flying machines. In fact, they've hardly arrived before an important-looking bird official bustles over towards the Brella, together with two guards. "How dare you bring that machine here!" it squawks. "The King has given strict instructions that anyone travelling by flying machine must be brought before him without delay. Guards, take them away!"

RUPERT'S FRIEND IS HAILED

The Sage and Rupert both bow low.
The King hates aeroplanes, they know!

"I know you're Rupert Bear, but who
Is this you've brought along with you?"

Rupert says, "He's the Sage of Um."
And starts to tell him why they've come . . .

"Stop!" laughs the King. "From what I hear,
The Sage is someone birds hold dear!"

The Bird King has already been told a flying machine has landed in his palace grounds and is looking extremely stern as Rupert and the Sage are marched in by the guards. "You, little bear!" he exclaims when he sees Rupert. "You are aware how much I detest flying machines. What is it that brings you here and why have you dared to risk my wrath?" Before Rupert can answer, he notices the Sage. "Who is this you have with you?" he demands.

"Your Majesty, this is my friend, the Sage of Um," Rupert replies. "We meant no offence by flying here in the Brella," he adds, but at the mention of the Sage's name the King's manner changes and he starts to smile. "The Sage of Um!" he exclaims. "For many years I have been hearing of how he and his Brella have so often helped birds in trouble, all of them my subjects." He turns to the Sage: "I have long wanted to thank you in person. But what is it I can do for you?"

"What brings you here? Please tell me how
I can be of help to you now . . ."

The Sage explains, but suddenly
The King cries, "No, this cannot be!"

He goes outside and leads the pair
Towards a tree that's growing there.

"The Dove of Dawn lives in this tree –
The large white dove which you can see . . ."

"There is indeed a great service you can perform for us," replies the Sage. "But it is something far greater than I have a right to ask. Yet I must, for it is the only way to break a wicked spell that has been cast on the child of a dear friend." "Name it!" cries the King. "We need tail feathers from your Dove of Dawn to make a fan," declares the Sage. "Only they will end the enchanted sleep of the Twilight Fan . . ." "Oh, no!" cries the King in despair. "This cannot be!"

A moment after his cry of dismay, the King regains his composure and apologises to the startled pair. "Come," he says. "You shall see how much you ask." He leads them out on to a terrace where there grows a single tree. Built into its spreading branches is a spacious bird-house, outside which is perched a large white dove. When the three get closer, Rupert notices that the bird's eyes are curiously gentle. "Unfold your tail for us," the King commands.

"It can't shed tail feathers for you
Because its tail has only two!"

"A single feather less then, why,
The poor bird couldn't even fly . . ."

"Then," shrugs the Sage, "our quest will fail.
The child must *be fanned by its tail!"*

The dove coos, "If it's as you say,
I'll give you feathers, come what may!"

"As your Majesty wishes," coos the Dove of Dawn, and turns to spread out its tail. The Sage and Rupert gasp with surprise, for it is made up of just two large feathers . . . "Now you see why I was so dismayed!" says the King. "To remove even *one* tail feather would mean that this, the rarest bird in the world, the Dove that wafts us to happy wakefulness each day, would never fly again. I cannot ask that of the poor creature. Surely you understand . . ."

Seeing how downcast Rupert and the Sage both look, the King asks gently, "Is there no other way to awaken your young friend than by making a fan from the Dove's tail?" "None," says the Sage. "If she is not fanned by its feathers she will sleep on and on." "For ever?" asks a soft voice. Rupert stares in astonishment for it is the Dove that has spoken. "As far as I know," nods the Sage. "Then I shall give up my tail," the dove coos. "The sleeping child must be saved."

RUPERT FINDS THE ANSWER

"To save the child, I'll lose my flight,"
The dove declares. "It's only right . . ."

The Bird King sighs, then walks away.
"Oh, very well then. As you say . . ."

The dove's tail wafts the scent of dawn
That wakens people every morn.

And slowly Rupert starts to find
The fragrance acts upon his mind.

Rupert and the Sage are lost for words. How can they ask so much from the Dove? Yet without its sacrifice poor Tigerlily will be doomed to sleep forever. The King looks grave. "Please, your Majesty!" the Dove pleads. "I must give up my tail if it's the only way to save this child . . . Summon the doctor immediately." The King nods glumly and leaves. As they wait for him to return, the dove coos softly and flutters its strange tail gently to and fro . . .

To Rupert's surprise, the Dove of Dawn does not seem alarmed but simply carries on fanning the air with its tail. As he watches the Dove, Rupert notices a sweet fragrance and asks, "What is that lovely smell?" "The waking scent that's wafted by my tail," coos the Dove. As he breathes in the scent, Rupert's mind becomes strangely clear. He suddenly remembers something tremendously important, just as the Bird King comes back across the terrace, accompanied by the doctor.

The King returns and says, "You see
I've brought the bird doctor with me."

The Dawn Dove doesn't hesitate,
But suddenly Rupert calls, "Wait!"

He asks the Sage, "That book you read,
Tell me *exactly what it said . . ."*

"Of course, Rupert! I understand.
It only said she must be fanned . . ."

The Dove flutters down to meet the King. The doctor looks solemn and the King glum. He speaks gently to the Dove: "Are you sure you want to do this?" "I have no choice," the Dove coos. "It must be done." The King does not speak for a long moment, then he nods to the doctor. The doctor opens his bag, but, at that very moment, Rupert cries out, "No, wait! I don't think the Dove has to lose its tail after all!" The others turn and stare at him in astonishment.

"How good is your memory?" Rupert asks the Sage. "Excellent," replies his friend. "Then tell me *exactly* what that book said would wake Tigerlily," Rupert goes on. The Sage looks puzzled, then starts to recite: "To be fanned using the tail feathers of the Dove of Dawn!" He turns to Rupert with a grin. "Why, of course! It said nothing about taking the feathers from the Dove . . . All we need is for the Dove to come back with us and fan Tigerlily with its tail!"

*"The dove can come with us and then
Wake Tigerlily up again!"*

*"Bravo!" the King cries happily.
"Its tail is saved! Now, follow me!"*

*He leads them to the courtyard where
The Sage's Brella's waiting there.*

*"Good luck!" the King cries and soon they
Are speeding off, upon their way.*

"Why didn't we think of this before?" asks the Sage. "Because we were too upset to think clearly," replies Rupert. "When I breathed in the waking scent from the Dove's tail feathers, my mind started working much faster than usual and I remembered exactly what the book of spells said." "Just in time!" chuckles the Sage. He turns to the King, and asks, "Your Majesty, may we borrow this very generous Dove?" "Of course!" cries the King. "You shall leave at once!"

He turns and leads the way back to the courtyard where the Sage's Brella was left. "Am I to ride in this?" coos the Dove. "What a treat!" "Do you think it is quite proper for a bird?" asks the King. "It will be much quicker this way," the Sage urges. "Very well," agrees the King. "But the Dove must fly back all by itself." "Farewell, your Majesty!" cries Rupert. "Thanks for all your help!" The Sage orders the Brella to fly to Nutwood, and off it soars, at top speed.

RUPERT BRINGS THE CURE

The dove's amazed how fast they go.
"My goodness! This makes birds seem slow."

The Brella swoops and Rupert sees
The tall pagoda, ringed with trees.

The Conjurer is startled when
He hears Rupert come back again.

"Good news!" the Sage cries cheerfully.
"I've brought the Dove of Dawn with me!"

"I'm glad you remembered in time what that book said about using my tail feathers," the Dove of Dawn tells Rupert from its perch on the Brella's handle. "I didn't fancy not being able to fly! Talking of which, I must say Brella-riding's much more fun than ordinary flying. It's a pity our King is so set against flying machines." "Hold on tight," the Sage tells it. "There's the Conjurer's pagoda where Rupert's friend, Tiger-lily, is fast asleep. Right then, down we go!"

The Brella has scarcely landed before Rupert leaps out and races into the pagoda. He finds the Conjurer kneeling beside the couch where Tigerlily is still sleeping soundly. "It's all right!" he cries. "We've found it!" "Found what?" the Conjurer blinks. "The means to break the spell of the Twilight Fan!" announces the Sage, striding into the room as the Dove flutters on ahead. "This splendid bird should have Tigerlily wide awake in no time!"

The Conjurer gasps, "All is well?
Then please, I beg you, break the spell!"

The dove takes off and quickly flies
To where poor Tigerlily lies.

It perches near and starts to fan
The strongest perfume that it can.

First Tigerlily smiles, then she
Begins to wake up happily.

"This bird?" cries the Conjurer. "Release my Tigerlily from that awful spell? I do not understand!" So the Sage explains what he found in the book of spells, about the Dove's willingness to help Tigerlily and how Rupert saved it from having to sacrifice its tail. "Then quickly, I beg you, undo the spell!" the Conjurer pleads. At these words, the Dove rises from the Sage's wrist, where it has been perching, and flies towards Tigerlily.

The Dove of Dawn settles gently on Tigerlily's couch. It coos softly and spreads out its strange tail. The two feathers quiver like a rapidly-waving fan. This time the waking scent is stronger and even lovelier than before. It almost seems to sparkle as it wafts towards Tigerlily's face. Everyone watches anxiously as Tigerlily starts to murmur softly in her sleep. She stirs, smiles gently, then her eyelids begin to flicker. "She's waking up!" cries Rupert.

RUPERT BIDS THE DOVE GOODBYE

She sits up with a start, then cries
As if she can't believe her eyes.

Her father smiles and starts to tell
How she was rescued from a spell.

He thanks the Dawn Dove gratefully.
"You've brought my daughter back to me!"

The dove explains that it must be
Home soon and leaves immediately.

As Tigerlily sits up slowly, her smile gives way to a puzzled frown – especially when she sees the Dove. "I don't understand . . ." she says in a bewildered voice. "But you soon shall!" cries the Conjurer, happily. "Welcome back!" Rupert and the Sage smile delightedly as the Dove flutters back to the Sage's wrist. When her father has finished telling her all that has happened, Tigerlily looks around at Rupert, the Sage and the cooing Dove. "Thank you all," she whispers.

The Conjurer begs Rupert and the others to tell them how he can reward them for what they have done. "It's enough to know that we were able to save your daughter," replies the Dove. "Hear, hear!" cry Rupert and the Sage. "And now I must be getting back to the Bird Kingdom," says the Dove. "I have to be home in time for tomorrow's dawn." And so the joyful party make their way outside. Goodbyes are said, the Dove flutters into the air, circles once and is gone.

73

"Will Tung-tai still try to harm you?"
"No! Now there's nothing he can do!"

The Sage and Rupert say goodbye,
Then sail across the Nutwood sky.

"There!" Mrs. Bear cries. "Look, you see,
I said they'd both be back for tea!"

How Rupert's parents marvel when
They hear the whole tale told again.

"But what about Tung-tai?" Rupert asks the Conjurer. "Won't he try to strike again?" "I think not," his friend replies. "In putting a spell on Tigerlily, he knows he has gone too far. Every magician's hand will be against him when they learn what he has done!" "He will be punished for his wickedness," adds the Sage, "We have no more to fear!" Rupert feels much happier now he knows Tung-tai is beaten. "I must go home and let Mummy know that Tigerlily is safe," he declares.

In no time at all, he and the Sage are back in the Brella, speeding towards Rupert's house. Mr. and Mrs. Bear are just about to go in for tea when Rupert and the Sage arrive. Mrs. Bear has told Rupert's father everything that's happened, and they are both anxious to hear if Tigerlily has been saved. "Yes!" cries Rupert and goes on to tell them the whole story. "Well," says Mrs. Bear as he finishes, "I must say I'm glad it worked out so happily after all!" The End.

Freddy the fox

Use a 5" to 7" square of paper white on one side black (or brown) on the other. Always check your fold in the next diagram.

1

2

3

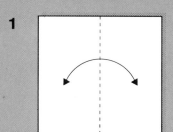

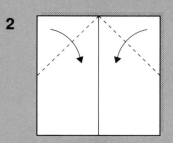

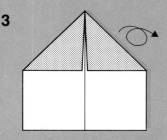

(1) White side up. Fold in half. Unfold. (2) Fold corners to centre line. (3) Turn model over - like turning a page in a book.

4

5

6

7

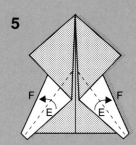

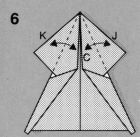

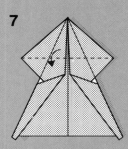

(4) Fold so edge 'A' lies along centre line 'C' let the flap underneath come out. Now do the same with 'B'. (5) Fold edge 'E' along 'F'.(both sides) (6) Fold edge 'J' along centre line 'C' and *open up* do the same with 'K' (7) Fold along dashed line.

8

9

10

11

12

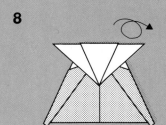

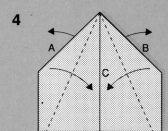

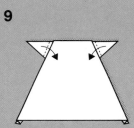

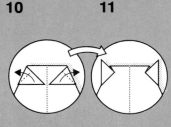

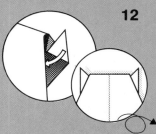

(8) Turn over like a page in a book. (9) Fold little flaps (ears) on dashed line. (10) Now fold the corners out again on dashed line. (11) This is the result now lift each ear and tuck *under* the top layer. (12) This is the ear being tucked under - do both now turn over.

(13) Fold up and crease on dashed line (about 1/3 of the way to the nose of the fox). (14) Hold each leg *below* the fold you made in step 13. Twist a little so your thumbs are on top and fingers below, now move the hands away from each other so the paper is tight - then bring the hands closer and Freddy will nod. (15) Move fingers together and then pull first one leg and then the other downwards, Freddy will put his head on one side.

13

15

14

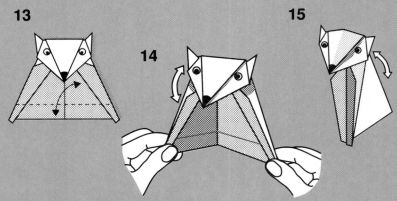

This design was created by John S Smith of the British Origami Society

Chatterbox

1

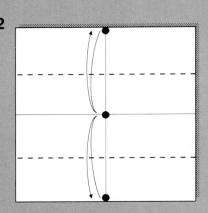

(1) Start with a 5" to 7" square of paper, coloured side down. Fold in half both ways and open out.
(2) Fold opposite sides to the centre crease and open out. Turn the paper over.

2

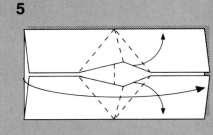

3

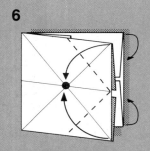

4

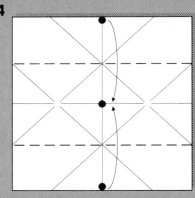

5

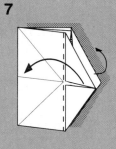

(3) Take each end of the lower quarter crease to where the vertical half-way meets the upper crease (dot to dot). Rotate the paper and repeat the two creases. Turn over.

(4) This should be your crease-pattern, if not, check the creases in step three. Fold the two edges back in to the centre.

(5) Using *only* creases you have already made, fold in half from left to right, opening up two small triangular pockets. Fold slowly and carefully here and do not force the paper.

6   **7**

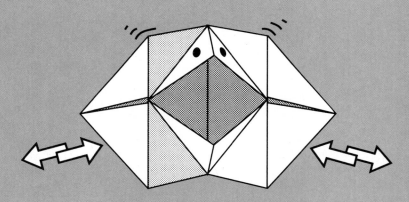

(6) Fold the two corners to meet the centre crease, repeat on the flap behind.
(7) Fold each of these corners backwards. Then hold each corner and gently pull them apart. Keep opening and closing to make the mouth chatter!

This design was created by Nick Robinson of the British Origami Society

Swan Candy Dish

1

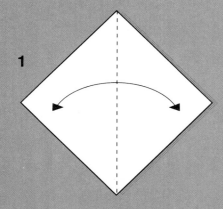

(1) Start with an 8" to 11" square piece of paper. Place it pretty side down, diamond position. Diagonal fold left corner to right corner. Unfold.

2

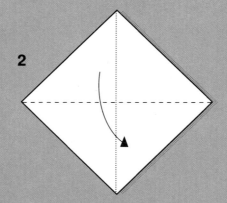

(2) Diagonal fold top corner to bottom corner.

3

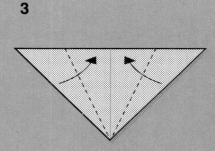

(3) Fold left and right double raw edges up to meet on vertical mountain crease.

4

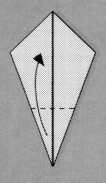

(4) Fold bottom tip up to horizontal folded edge hidden under wings.

5

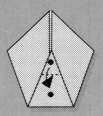

(5) Fold same tip down to lie halfway between the two horizontal folded edges.

6

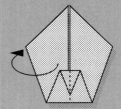

(6) Mountain fold left half of model around behind to match right half.

7

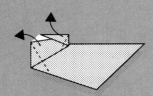

(7) Pull neck away from body to desired angle and set by firmly pressing folded edges flat at bottom left. Similarly pull head away from neck, etc.

8

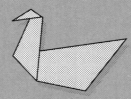

(8) Open and shape the hollow wings to hold the goodies.

This design was created by Laura Kruskal of the British Origami Society

RUPERT and

*Here's Rika, Rupert's Lapp friend, who
Is staying for a day or two.*

When Santa's reindeer aren't pulling his sleigh at Christmas, they live in Lapland, where they are looked after by a little girl called Rika. Rupert and Rika are good friends and have agreed that she will stop off on her journey home to spend a day or two in Nutwood. Rupert's parents are delighted to see her when she arrives late one evening, having left her reindeer tied up in Pong-Ping's garden, where there's plenty of room.

the Stolen Snowmen

The reindeer herd she had to bring
Are being cared for by Pong-Ping.

"Tomorrow," Rupert says, "we should
Be able to explore Nutwood."

Later that evening, when Rupert and Rika take a last look out of the window before going to their rooms, the night is clear and moonlight glistens on the snow. "Doesn't it look lovely," smiles Rupert. "Yes," agrees Rika, "so calm and still." Long after the pair have said goodnight and gone to bed, Rupert is woken by the howling of the wind. Instead of calm moonlight outside, he sees thick snow flashing past his bedroom window . . .

But in the night it starts to snow
And howling winds begin to blow . . .

RUPERT SPOTS BILLY BLIZZARD

Rupert peers out, then rubs his eyes
As past his room, a snowman flies!

Then Rupert sees someone he knows
Who seems to guide the raging snows . . .

"It's Billy Blizzard!" Rupert cries
As off the frosty figure flies.

"Whatever's wrong?" asks Mrs. Bear.
"It's Billy Blizzard! He's out there!"

Rupert jumps out of bed and opens the window. It is almost snatched from his grasp by the swirling white storm which rages outside. He peers out and gives a cry of amazement as he sees his snowman, which has been standing in the garden, caught up by the storm and carried away on the wind. As the snowman spins past his window, the storm seems to clear and Rupert sees a familiar-looking figure standing outside, directing the snow with a jagged icicle.

"It's Billy Blizzard!" Rupert's cry rings out above the noise of the wind, and the sinister figure turns to give him a wicked grin. The next minute he leaps up after the tail of the snowstorm and is carried away into the night. "Rupert! Whatever's the matter? Do shut that window!" says Mrs. Bear, who has heard Rupert call out. Rika has heard him too and comes to see what's happening. "It was Billy Blizzard!" Rupert cries. "I saw him out there, standing in the garden."

RUPERT AND RIKA SEE JACK FROST

*"He's Jack Frost's cousin who was sent
To the South Pole as punishment."*

*"He's gone and there's no damage done
So back to bed now everyone . . ."*

*Next morning Rupert's keen to show
Rika the sights, so off they go.*

*"Look!" Rupert cries, amazed as they
See Jack Frost almost straightaway . . .*

"Who's Billy Blizzard?" asks Rika. Rupert explains that he's Jack Frost's cousin, who was banished to the Frozen South by Jack's father, King Frost, because he kept making terrifying blizzards. "Ever since then, he's been a sworn enemy of the King. That was one of his blizzards just now. It was so strong that it carried off my snowman!" "Well, there's nothing we can do about it now," says Mrs. Bear. "Back to bed, everybody. Try to get a good night's sleep."

Next morning Rupert and Rika agree not to spoil the first day of her visit by worrying about Billy Blizzard. As soon as they have finished breakfast, they set off to have a proper look round Nutwood. No one is about as they head across the common to the top of a hill from where, Rupert tells Rika, you can see the whole of the village. They are almost there when Rupert spots somebody scanning the horizon with a telescope. "Look!" he cries. "It's Jack Frost."

He turns around and greets the pair
Then tells them what he's doing there.

"I've come to look for snowmen, though
It seems that Nutwood's none to show!"

"That's Billy Blizzard's work, I'm sure!"
Gasps Rupert and tells what he saw . . .

"Each year Jack takes them to the King –
Now Blizzard's ruined everything!"

Jack is so intent on studying Nutwood through his telescope that he doesn't notice Rika and Rupert until they reach the top of the hill. "Why, Rupert!" he exclaims. "I was just about to try and find you. But who's this?" Rupert introduces Rika, who says she's delighted to meet Jack Frost at last. "What did you want me for?" Rupert asks. "I hoped you'd be able to tell me what's happened to all the snowmen around here," says Jack. "There's not a single one to be seen!"

"I can tell you what happened to *my* snowman!" Rupert cries. As he hears about last night's blizzard, Jack Frost looks more and more grim. "It's plain that Billy has taken them all to get back at my father," he declares. Rika looks bewildered, so Rupert explains that each year, just before the thaw, Jack comes to collect all the snowmen and take them to his father's palace. "Now I've got to find a way to get this year's snowmen back from Billy Blizzard!" says Jack.

RUPERT'S PAL RIKA HAS A PLAN

*"I'll have to try and get them back
From Billy's fortress!" declares Jack.*

*They'll all go there, the three decide
On Santa's reindeer, which they'll ride.*

*It's all arranged, but even so
Rupert must ask if he may go.*

*"Of course you may," says Mrs. Bear.
"But keep warm if it's chilly there."*

Jack explains that he's sure Billy Blizzard has taken the missing snowmen to his ice fortress in the Frozen South. "The trouble is, I can't call up a wind to fly there as it's the wrong part of the world . . ." "I'm sure Santa wouldn't mind you borrowing his reindeer," Rika suggests. "You mean you'd really lend them to me?" cries Jack. "Of course, I'd have to come too," says Rika, "to make sure they're all right." "Then so must I," declares Rupert, stoutly.

Although he's keen to join the others, Rupert knows that he has to ask his mother first. "I'll come with you," says Jack as Rika hurries off to Pong-Ping's house to get the reindeer ready. Mrs. Bear has met Jack Frost before and knows that Rupert has always returned safely from their adventures together. When she hears what's happened, and that Rika will be going too, she agrees to let Rupert go and help Jack but tells him to wrap up well.

RUPERT SETS OFF WITH HIS CHUMS

Then Jack and Rupert run to reach
Pong-Ping's to choose a reindeer each . . .

"I've got two saddled up for you,"
Says Rika, who checks her lasso.

The pals are ready to depart:
At Rika's word their flight will start . . .

"Hold tight now!" Rika warns as they
Take off, then calls, "Up and away!"

Rupert and Jack hurry to Pong-Ping's house where Rika has prepared three of her reindeer for the long flight to the Frozen South. Her face lights up when she hears that Rupert can come too. Pong-Ping has agreed to look after the other reindeer and is introducing himself to Jack Frost when Rupert notices that Rika is tying a coil of rope to her saddle. "What's that?" he asks her. "A reindeer herdsman's lasso," Rika replies. "I always carry it with me on a long journey."

Daylight is fading by the time Rupert and the others are ready to set off. The reindeer usually fly only at night because Santa prefers them not to be seen. But since Pong-Ping's house is well away from the village and as it's nearly dark already, Rika agrees that this time they may start straightaway. "Good luck!" cries Pong-Ping as the three chums mount up. "Up and away!" calls Rika and in no time at all the three reindeer are soaring up into the darkening sky.

RUPERT SEES A STRANGE STAR

Jack leads the way through starry skies
To where his cousin's fortress lies.

"Look!" Rika cries as a strange light
Flies towards them through the dark night . . .

"A shooting star?" asks Jack. But no,
It can't be for it's far too slow.

Then Rupert gasps aloud and blinks:
Can the strange light be what he thinks?

Night falls and soon Rupert has the feeling he is flying among the stars. Although Rika is in charge of the reindeer it is Jack Frost who decides upon their course. "How can you be so sure you're right?" Rupert asks him. "When my father banished Billy Blizzard he exiled him to the Frozen South," says Jack. "I know where . . ." Before he can finish Rika breaks in with a cry of, "Look! There's a strange light ahead of us. What can it be? It seems to be coming this way!"

"Perhaps it's a shooting star?" suggests Jack. "Then it's like none I've ever seen," answers Rika as the light weaves its way towards them. "Too slow and wobbly." To Rupert's surprise the light seems oddly familiar and as it gets closer a thought grows in his mind. "It couldn't be, surely," he whispers. "What did you say?" asks Rika. But Rupert is too excited to answer. For now he is sure he knows what the strange light is. "How extraordinary!" he gasps. "It *is* him!"

*"The Sage of Um!" laughs Rupert, "Why,
It's his lamp we saw in the sky!"*

*How does a Nutwood snowman come
To be there with the Sage of Um?*

*"A blizzard blew past suddenly
And dropped him here, right next to me!"*

*The snowman asks if they can go
To Nutwood but the Sage says no.*

"The Sage of Um!" cries Rupert. His friends see that the light is really a lantern hanging from the handle of a large, upturned umbrella in which sits an old man dressed in a long gown. "An unexpected pleasure!" smiles the Sage as Rupert introduces him to Rika and Jack, explaining that the Sage is an old friend. "It's been a night of strange meetings," laughs the Sage and gestures to the snowman who's sitting alongside him. "You'll never guess how I met him!"

It turns out that the Sage was flying towards his home on the island of Um when a blizzard suddenly appeared from nowhere. "I dived down to get out of the way," he explains, "but scraped the underneath of the storm cloud. That's when this snowman appeared. Must have fallen out of the cloud. What am I to do with him?" "Take me back to Nutwood," pipes up the Snowman. "I'm afraid I can't," says the Sage. "I have to get back to Um island without delay."

RUPERT IS JOINED BY A SNOWMAN

The Sage must fly to Um, so Jack
Says they will take the snowman back.

The snowman manages to climb
On Rupert's reindeer in no time.

Then, waving everyone goodbye,
The Sage soars off across the sky.

The snowman learns where they are bound
And begs Rupert to turn around.

"What's the matter?" asks Rupert. "It's the unicorns!" replies the Sage, who looks after the only unicorn herd in the whole world. "They've all caught bad colds, I'm afraid. I've got to get back and make sure that they're all right." "In that case we'll take the snowman," says Jack. "He ought to be with me, anyway." "He can ride on my reindeer," says Rupert and flies closer to the Brella. The snowman smiles and eagerly clambers up behind Rupert.

"Nice to meet you!" calls the Sage as he whisks away. We must hurry," says Jack. "Forward!" cries Rika and off bound the reindeer. "No! Wait!" squeaks the snowman. "There must be a mistake! This is the way Billy Blizzard went!" "Of course!" says Rupert. "We're going after him to make him give back the snowmen he stole from Nutwood . . ." "But I've just got away from him," whimpers the snowman. "He might catch me again. Oh, no don't go on, please!"

RUPERT ARRIVES AT BILLY'S FORT

"We can't," says Jack, "until we free
The other snowmen, don't you see!"

Just then the sky begins to glow,
For Blizzard's fortress lies below.

Around the fort the three friends see
A snowstorm rages constantly . . .

"He'll see us if we fly too near,"
Says Jack. "Let's land and walk from here."

"How selfish!" thinks Rupert. "I'm glad he isn't mine." "Please turn back, Jack Frost!" begs the snowman. "I don't want to be one of Billy Blizzard's slaves." "Nor do the other snowmen he stole!" snaps Jack. "Can't *you* get him to turn back?" the snowman appeals to Rupert and Rika. But neither replies for, in the growing light, they can see something ahead. "Can that be . . . ?" Rika begins. "Yes," Jack says quietly. "It's Billy Blizzard's stronghold."

The reindeer slow to a halt. The whimpering of the snowman is the only sound as Rupert and the others gaze at the grim ice fortress, which is surrounded by a moat bristling with spears of ice. The only entrance is over a drawbridge, which is firmly closed. There is no chance of flying in on the reindeer, for a constant blizzard swirls fiercely above the walls. "We must land somewhere out of sight and decide what to do," says Jack. The snowman gives a low moan.

RUPERT HAS AN IDEA

They circle low, until they find
Some ice slabs they can hide behind.

"Come on!" calls Jack and scrambles to
The top to get a better view.

How can they get inside the fort
To free the snowmen who've been caught?

Then Rupert has a good idea,
"We'll get Blizzard to come out here!"

"We'd be out of sight down there," says Rupert, pointing to a flat stretch of snow behind some ice slabs which face Billy Blizzard's fortress. The snowman groans. Jack, though, agrees with Rupert, so Rika leads the way down in a wide sweep and lands behind the ridge of ice. The three friends dismount at once and scramble up to the top in order to spy out the land. The snowman stays put, dismally gazing after them and snivelling quietly to himself.

When they reach the top of the ridge, Rupert, Rika and Jack gaze glumly at the sight that greets them. Between the ice slabs and the fortress is a stretch of open ground, then a moat, filled with ice spears. Above the walls a blizzard rages wildly. "I just can't see a way of getting in," Jack sighs. "Nor can I," declares Rika. "We may not have to get *in* at all," says Rupert. "All we need to do to free the snowmen is make Billy Blizzard come *out*."

RUPERT PLEADS WITH THE SNOWMAN

"But how?" asks Jack. Rupert replies,
"We'll lure him with a tempting prize!"

"A snowman!" cries Jack. "Yes, I see!
But do you think ours will agree?"

"Oh, no!" the snowman wails, "You can't
Use me as bait. You won't, I shan't!"

"Please!" Rupert says, "It's up to you
To help us free the others too!"

"How?" asks Jack. "We have to tempt him," says Rupert and points to the dismal snowman waiting below. "I'm sure Billy Blizzard won't be able to resist a chance to recapture the prisoner he lost on the way from Nutwood!" "But that cowardly snowman will never agree to act as bait!" says Rika. "We must try!" says Jack. "Our only hope is to lure Billy out, then grab him and make him hand over all the snowmen. "Come on," he calls. "Let's make a start!"

The snowman is aghast when he hears Rupert's plan. "You must be potty!" he gasps. "I only just escaped being one of his slaves!" Seeing that the others are about to lose their tempers with the timid snowman, Rupert makes a last appeal for help. "I know it's asking an awful lot," he says, "but it's the only way your fellow snowmen can be saved from a miserable life of slavery under a cruel and wicked master." The snowman gulps but says nothing.

RUPERT WATCHES ANXIOUSLY

The snowman thinks, then gives a sigh –
"You're right!" he says. "I have to try!"

As soon as Blizzard comes in sight
Rika's lasso will bind him tight.

The others watch the snowman who
Gets ready to step into view.

He nears the fort and then they see
The drawbridge crash down suddenly . . .

The snowman stares at his feet for a long time. Then he looks up at Rupert. "All right!" he says. "But I'm still scared." "Heroes often are," says Jack. "Me?" the snowman scoffs. "Not a heroic snowflake in my body." So it's agreed: the snowman will show himself on the open stretch of snow in front of the fortress. "Wait a moment," Rupert says. "What if Billy Blizzard runs inside again as soon as he sees us?" "Just let him try!" says Rika and reaches for her reindeer lasso.

Rupert and the others get into position and watch anxiously as the snowman slowly edges his way down to the open stretch of snow, keeping to the shadows as long as he can. He has been told to go just far enough into the open for Billy Blizzard to be able to see him. He pauses in the shadows at the foot of the slabs. Has he lost his nerve? No. He steps into the open and waits. For a long time nothing happens. Then, with a loud crash, the drawbridge slams down over the moat . . .

91

RUPERT'S PLAN WORKS

Next minute there's an angry shout
As Billy Blizzard charges out!

Rika lassos him expertly
But slips as Blizzard tries to flee.

The timid snowman saves the day
And stops him as he gets away!

As soon as Blizzard's safely tied
Up tight, Jack says, "Let's go inside!"

Over the drawbridge charges a furious Billy Blizzard. He brandishes an icicle dart but the snowman stands his ground. Rupert and the others, who have been crouching out of sight, jump up into view. Billy casts them a wild glance but, before he can do anything, Rika swings her lasso round in the air and drops it over his shoulders. He squeals and starts to run back to the drawbridge, jerking Rika off her feet and dragging her along with him.

Rupert and Jack scramble after Rika to try and rescue her. They needn't worry though, for the snowman launches himself at Billy, bowling him over and sending his icicle dart flying. Rika picks herself up and the others join her. In no time at all Billy Blizzard has been soundly trussed up. Jack hauls him to his feet and points towards the stronghold. "We're all going inside now," he snaps. "And you're coming with us, whether you like it or not!"

92

RUPERT SEES THE SNOWMEN FREED

Inside the fort Jack takes a key
And goes to set the snowmen free.

Then Rupert hears a mighty cheer
As all the prisoners appear.

"You may have set them free, but how,"
Sneers Blizard, "will you get home now?"

"Don't worry!" Rika smiles, "We'll cope.
Tied scarves will make a splendid rope!"

Billy Blizzard snarls with rage but lets himself be led into the fortress. "Where are the snowmen?" demands Jack, taking a set of keys from the pouch on Billy's belt. Billy nods towards a nearby door. Jack unlocks it and goes through, together with the snowman. It's hard to see how Billy could look any angrier, but he scowls even more as a great cheer comes from the other room. Out march a gaggle of snowmen, with Jack and the brave snowman perched on their shoulders.

Although he's been outsmarted, Billy Blizzard isn't finished yet. As the cheering dies down he turns to Jack and sneers, "Very clever. But how will you get the snowmen to your father's palace? You can't just summon a wind like you would in the top half of the world!" "Don't worry, Jack!" cries Rika. "We'll go back to Nutwood the way we came . . ." The pals look puzzled, but Rika has a plan. "Collect the snowmen's scarves and knot them into three ropes," she calls.

RUPERT'S PAL RIKA SAVES THE DAY

*She brings the reindeer near and then
Calls, "Now all come outside again!"*

*"I understand!" cries Rupert, "You
Plan to tow all the snowmen too!"*

*The snowmen stand where they are told
So each one has a "rope" to hold . . .*

*Jack leaves a dart deliberately
For Blizzard to cut himself free.*

Mystified by Rika's request, Rupert and Jack hurry to do as she asks while she brings the reindeer round to the flat area in front of the fort. Then, as everyone looks on, she ties a scarf "rope" to each of the reindeer's saddles. "Now I understand!" cries Rupert. "We're going to tow the snowmen all the way back to Nutwood!" "That's right," laughs Rika. "The reindeer will do it easily. A few snowmen weigh next to nothing, compared with Santa's loaded sleigh."

At last all is ready for the journey back to Nutwood, where Jack will be able to summon a wind to carry him and the snowmen on to King Frost's palace. The snowmen are split into three groups and each given a "rope" to hold. Before climbing onto his reindeer, Jack takes Billy Blizzard's icicle dart and sticks it upright in the snow. "You can cut yourself free as soon as we've gone," he tells him. "Don't try to follow us or you'll have my father's ice guards to deal with!"

RUPERT FLIES BACK TO NUTWOOD

Then Rika gives a rousing cry
And all the reindeer start to fly . . .

"We'll fly to Nutwood first," says Jack,
"And then I'll take the snowmen back."

"We're almost there now!" Rupert cries.
And points down to where Nutwood lies.

The reindeer slowly circle round,
Then gently settle on the ground.

"Ready?" asks Rika. Rupert and Jack nod and she gives a shrill cry. The reindeer start trotting across the flat snow, gradually gathering speed until they bound into the air, towing the snowmen behind them. "Nutwood next stop!" laughs Rupert as they race through the sky. "The snowmen and I will go straight on as soon as we arrive in Nutwood," says Jack. "I'm afraid I'll have to go home soon too," adds Rika. "I've got to get the reindeer back to Lapland."

The light begins to grow and after a while Rupert starts to recognise the landscape down below. "Nutwood!" he cries and points excitedly to the village. "Make sure you land on the high common," says Jack. "We don't want anyone to see." Rika nods and down they start to go. The reindeer land so gently that all the snowmen are able to keep their feet as they slowly touch down. "We made it!" shouts Rupert happily. Everyone grins with delight, even the snowmen.

RUPERT BIDS RIKA FAREWELL

It's time for Jack to go now so
He gives his wind whistle a blow.

A wind starts as he waves goodbye
And whisks the snowmen through the sky.

Soon Rika must be on her way,
"I'll come back next year, if I may . . ."

"Yes!" Pong-Ping cries. "And then you'll see
The rest of Nutwood properly!"

Jack wastes no time in gathering the snowmen around him. Then he turns to Rika and Rupert and thanks them for all their help. "Thanks from my father too!" he calls as he bids them a final farewell. "I know he will be grateful for everything you've done." Taking a tiny whistle from the pouch on his belt, he gives the snowmen a sign to get ready. As soon as he blows the whistle a great wind starts to blow and whisks all the snowmen up into the air and out of sight.

That evening, as soon as it is dark, it is Rika's turn to say goodbye. She has already thanked Rupert's parents and is back in Pong-Ping's garden, ready to leave. "You really must come for a longer visit next time," Pong-Ping urges her. "I promise I shall," Rika laughs and mounts her reindeer. "Up and away!" she cries and blows a kiss to the two pals as the whole herd takes off into the night sky. "She *is* nice!" sigh Pong-Ping and Rupert together. THE END

Rupert's Memory Test

Please don't try this test until you have read all the stories in the book. When you have read them, study the pictures below. Each is part of a bigger picture you will have seen in a story. When you have done that, see if you can answer the questions at the bottom of the page. Afterwards check the stories to discover if you were right.

CAN YOU REMEMBER . . .

1. Who lives in this house?
2. What has this man heard?
3. Whose car is this?
4. Who has lowered this drawbridge?
5. What is Rupert looking for?
6. Why is this bird white?
7. What is splashing in this pool?
8. Who is this?

9. What are these men carrying?
10. Who lives here?
11. Who has sent this note?
12. Who is Rupert speaking to?
13. What is Jack Frost doing?
14. Where is this castle?
15. What have Rupert and Bill just seen?
16. Whose castle is this

RUPERT

Rupert Library
A classic collection of much loved Rupert stories, building into a wonderful library to keep forever.
Ideal for children aged: 4 – 8 years

Rupert Storytime
A bright and colourful series of new Rupert stories. Written in bold simple text, these books are ideal for parents to read to young children, or for early readers.
Ideal for children aged: 3 – 7 years

Rupert Mini Board Books
For very young Rupert readers. A delightful series of chunky board books, with clear bold text and beautiful illustrations.
Ideal for children aged: 6 months and upwards

Rupert Surprise Flap Books
New and original Rupert stories are combined with a 'lift the flap' technique to provide a colourful and exciting series of story books.
Ideal for children aged: 3 – 7 years

These and other Rupert books are available through all good bookshops. Contact Books Department, Express Newspapers plc, Ludgate House, 245 Blackfriars Road, London SE1 9UX for more information.

ANSWERS TO PUZZLE:
Spot the Difference: (page 52) 1. Bell missing from top of cupboard; 2. Picture missing from frame; 3. Lock missing from door; 4. Stamp missing from envelope; 5. Button missing from Mr. Bear's waistcoat; 6. Pattern missing from cereal packet; 7. Saucer missing; 8. Spoon missing from jam pot; 9. Spout missing from tea pot; 10. Rupert's glass missing; 11. Slat missing from back of chair.

Origami:
If you have enjoyed the origami pages you can find out more about the British Origami Society by writing to its secretary, Dave Brill at the following address:
British Origami Society, 253 Park Lane, Poynton, Stockport, Cheshire SK12 1RH.

Follow **Rupert** every day in the **Daily Express**